Smith's
MONTHLY

Every Month Original
Novels, Stories, and Articles

USA Today Bestselling Writer
Dean Wesley Smith

TABLE OF CONTENTS

SHORT STORIES

FULL NOVEL

SERIAL NOVEL

NONFICTION

Smith's Monthly Issue #32

Introduction
A BASICS ISSUE

This is the 32nd issue, so the 32nd month doing this magazine. I am proud of that record and want to keep it going.

And I could have only done this for thirty-two months with all your support, both as subscribers or on Patreon or just buying an issue from one of the many stores it is offered in. That support helps more than you can know.

On my blog, I talk at times about origins of my writing. Both readers and other writers tend to find that interesting.

So this issue has a focus on that.

The short Poker Boy novel in this issue was serialized in these pages, but as with all serial novels here, in a later issue I publish the entire thing so that those of you who don't like serial stories can read it all at once.

So the basis of this issue is that short novel.

As for the history of that, the short novel comes as a sequel to the only full Poker Boy novel I have written so far. It was that novel that started Poker Boy with his team and when he met his girlfriend, Front Desk Girl.

So even though the story was written a ways after the Poker Boy series had been going, it harks back to that very first origin novel.

Also in this issue are numbers of stories from my challenge last July. As I write this, I am planning on another short story challenge for July this year.

So I looked at the stories from last year's challenge and saw numbers of stories that over this last year formed the basis for full novels. So I thought I would include the basis stories in this issue to let you see how stories bloom into novels.

"A Bad Patch of Humanity" short story that starts off the issue expanded out into the Seeder's Universe novel *Star Mist* that was in issue twenty-five.

The next story, "A Great First Day," ended up as part of the Ghost of a Chance novel *Heaven Painted as a Cop Car* that was in issue twenty-three.

Thanks for the Support

Dean Wesley Smith

"The Problem of Grapevine Springs" and the "Idanha Hotel" short stories scattered in this issue both ended up in Thunder Mountain novels by the same names *(Grapevine Springs* and *The Idanha Hotel)* in issue twenty-seven and issue thirty.

"Make Myself Just One More" started off the novel *Death Finds a Partner* that was in issue thirty-one.

There are more short stories in this issue as well, the largest numbers of short stories in an issue so far.

I hope you enjoy the peek into how books come about, sometimes starting from the gems of short stories.

Thanks for being part of all this.

—Dean Wesley Smith
Lincoln City, Oregon
May 12, 2016

Coming Next Issue in *Smith's Monthly*
THE TAFT RANCH
A Thunder Mountain Novel

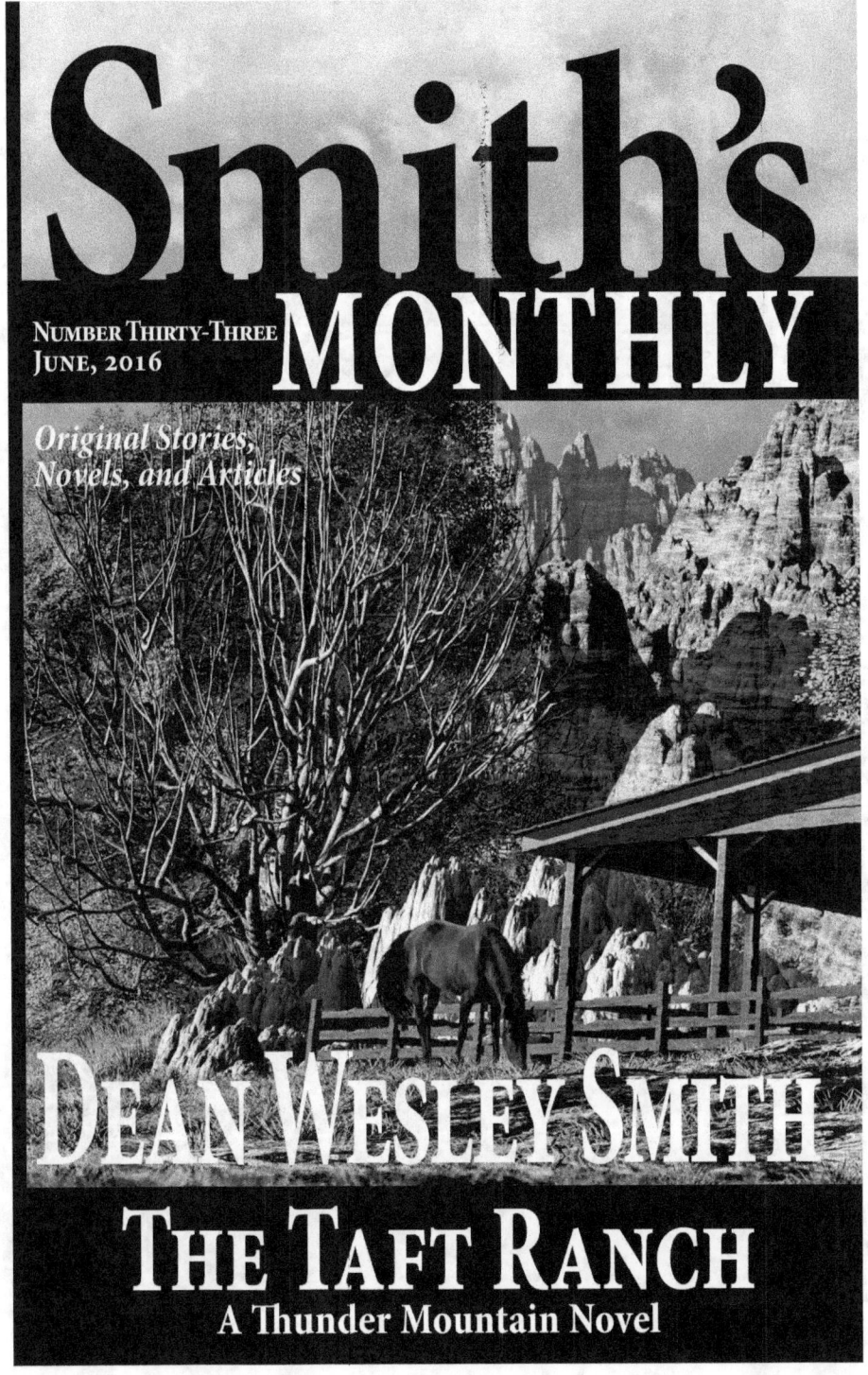

DEAN WESLEY SMITH

A BAD PATCH OF HUMANITY

A Seeders Universe Story

Most of humanity died one ugly day four years before. Now the survivors wanted to rebuild.

Angie Park's job consisted of telling survivors outside of Portland, Oregon, of the plans to rebuild. But some survivors wanted nothing to do with civilization.

And some thought killing worth the price to pay to stay alone.

In the galaxy-spanning Seeders Universe, "A Bad Patch of Humanity" focuses down on an early event in Angie Park's life, an event that starts her on her path to becoming a woman of legend in a hundred galaxies.

A BAD PATCH OF HUMANITY
A Seeders Universe Story

ONE

ANGIE PARK LET the sounds of her motorcycle die off into the silence of the forest and the ruins around her. Nothing moved, not even a slight breeze among the tall pines and the deserted general store and gas station tucked back into the trees.

The building had been cute at one point in the past, almost like a cottage, but now the paint was peeling, the windows were covered in grime, and weeds were growing thick between the building and the useless gas pump. On one side blackberries were starting to crawl up a wall and in a few years would bury the old building.

She had parked on the edge of the two-lane road that wound up through the Cascade Mountains. The road in this area had been still in good shape and very few car wrecks had blocked her for the last twenty miles since she had left I-5.

She pulled off her helmet and let her long black hair fall over her shoulders as she dismounted and set the helmet on her leather supply pack. She had a small saddle rifle in a sling on her back and a small caliber gun hidden in a holster on her leg under her jeans.

Her light jacket covered a T-shirt and she unzipped the jacket to let in the fresh mountain air. It was early summer and the heat today was predicted to be around ninety by the middle of the afternoon, even this high in the mountains.

Around her the silence of the Oregon forest seemed to press in, but after all the years of being alone, she was used to silence more than the noise of being around other people. That's why she had volunteered for this task, to go out and tell others about Portland.

Plus she really believed in what Portland was building and wanted everyone to know.

Up a small dirt road in front of her that wound through the tall pine trees, she knew a compound sat at the top of that road with six people living in it. Six survivors of the Event, as it was now being called.

The Event had been a wave of electromagnetic energy that swept over the Earth just over three years ago. It hadn't hurt equipment, but it had killed any exposed humans and dogs and horses and a few other animals. Thankfully it spared cats because she didn't know what she would have done the first few years of being alone without her cats to keep her company.

Humans who had survived were like her. They happened to be underground or in a vault of some type and were protected from the invisible but deadly wave. She had been a Professor of Physics at the University of Oregon and had been three stories down in a lab under the physics department when the Event happened. Millions like her had survived worldwide, and now civilization was working to rebuild.

She had been living far up the Columbia Gorge in a home overlooking the river to get away from the smell of all the dying bodies. She had discovered that civilization was rebuilding when convoy after convoy of motorcycles went down the freeway below her home headed for Portland in the spring of the second year. Men, women, and children.

Because of its climate and natural resources, Portland had been picked as one of the five cities to be the center of the new world in this country. She had followed the convoys after a time and saw and listened to what they were doing and trying to build. A month later she had packed up her cats and moved to Portland to try to help.

Now she was doing what they called "outreach" to those who hadn't heard yet about building the new world. It was dangerous, but she had wanted to do it. A couple of her friends had insisted she not go alone, but she had felt that a woman alone would be more convincing than a bunch of people. So far, she had been right about that.

Since so many of the military had survived on ships, submarines, underground compounds, all the top science had survived as well and was being used in the rebuild. She had seen satellite photos of the compound at the end of the dirt road that was her next stop for the day.

She knew that six were living there. They had set up electrical and had running water to most of their buildings and had a pretty decent surveillance system set up that more than likely was watching her now.

That's why she had stopped here, to let them watch her. Last thing she needed to do was surprise anyone who had been surviving and living off of nature for three years. Doing that could get a person really dead really quickly.

Over the years, it seemed that a lot of people had gone completely insane thinking that civilization was gone and that they were left alone.

She had thought at one point she might go insane as well because death was just everywhere. The very reason she had found a place on the top of a hill was for protection from the nut cases roaming around, and to avoid the smell of death that first year. But she had set that home up so she could protect it. Luckily, she never had had to.

She looked up the dirt road that wound into the tall pines. It looked far cooler than where she was standing now near the highway in the sun. She needed to get moving.

She knew the names of four of the six people who were living there. And knew that two of them had surviving family members.

Of the thirty compounds like this one she had approached over the last six months, most had come into the city later on their own terms, and after that many had moved into town, just as she had done.

But others were happy where they were and she respected that.

Her job wasn't to convince them to join humanity again, but to just let them know what was happening.

She took a long cool drink from her canteen, put it back on her bike, then with

her hands in the air, started up the road toward the compound. Walking like that told the people watching she knew she was being watched and only wanted to talk.

At least she hoped that's what it told them.

TWO

IT TOOK HER ten minutes to walk up the dirt road before she crested over a slight ridge. She was sweating and now wished she had brought along her canteen instead of leaving it on the bike. It wasn't much after ten in the morning and it was already getting hot.

And walking with her hands in the air was never an easy task, especially going uphill as she had been doing.

Ahead she could see the five buildings of the compound, all well-maintained. Three single-story houses and two tall-peaked barns sat in a cluster with some fenced-in chicken areas to one side. The fences on those were tall and strung between solid poles, more than likely in an attempt to keep out mountain lions that roamed these hills.

She kept her hands in the air and kept walking toward the compound.

After another hundred paces, a man and two women stepped out of one house and moved to meet her. All three carried rifles, but had them cradled in their arms or down in one hand.

The woman on the right Angie recognized as Bettie Collins from photos. The woman on the left was her sister Bonnie. They had both lived in a small town to the east of here. She had no idea how they survived the Event. They must have been in a deep basement or something at the time as Angie had been.

The tall, very thin man in the middle Angie didn't recognize, but he looked to be about her age at thirty and had intelligence in his eyes that didn't seem to miss anything.

She instantly had a bad feeling about him. Instantly.

That was unusual.

None of them seemed at all worried about meeting a stranger. That wasn't normal in these situations either.

All three of them were dressed in jeans, light shirts, and work boots and all their clothing looked new and clean.

As they got within ten steps, the three stopped and Bettie signaled for Angie to stop and she did.

She was about ten yards from the tree line and very much out in the open.

"Put your arms down," Bettie said. "That had to be hard walking like that."

Angie did, smiling and rubbing her shoulders. "I've done it numbers of times, but it never gets that much easier. I'm Angela Park, but everyone just calls me Angie."

"Everyone," the man asked, clearly puzzled and not introducing himself at all.

Angie nodded. "That's what I'm here to tell you about. Civilization is slowly rebuilding. Portland is one of the five cities picked to be one of the centers. I'm just out trying to inform everyone about what is happening."

"How many people are in Portland?" Bettie asked.

Angie shrugged. "Last count about forty thousand."

"Forty thousand," Bonnie said, breathlessly.

The man didn't even flinch.

Angie nodded. "And your Aunt Carol is there and knew I was coming out this way and told me to send her best wishes. She survived as well."

Angie thought both Bettie and Bonnie were going to collapse right there, but both managed to take deep breaths and then look at each other.

Angie was starting to feel that something was off here. She wasn't sure, but her little voice was starting to get worried. These people were not reacting in the way that survivors on their own normally reacted, which was usually with

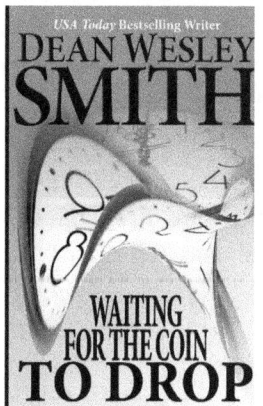

fear and then relief that civilization was rebuilding.

"Since civilization destroyed itself one time," the man said, "why is everyone so fired up to rebuild?"

"Humans had nothing to do with the Event," Angie said. "It was an electromagnetic wave that came out of deep space and swept over the entire planet. The scientists who knew it was coming thought it would be harmless. Turns out it was at a certain frequency that fried something in our human brains and everyone who wasn't either underground or protected behind steel died instantly and painlessly. It did not harm equipment."

"How do you know all this?" he asked.

"May I?" she asked, pointing to her back pocket.

He nodded and didn't raise his rifle.

He should have raised his rifle.

Something was very off.

As she pulled out three folded sheets and offered them to him, she glanced around looking for the three others who lived here to be in positions to kill her at the guy's signal. If they wanted to, she was as good as dead. She was a good ten running steps from the nearest shelter.

Bettie stepped forward and took the sheets, then stepped back and looked at the papers, handing them to the others one at a time.

"That information was recorded from the International Space Station," Angie said, staying on her practiced patter. "We finally got the men who were up there down a year ago, and used a couple existing rockets to resupply them in the meantime."

All three looked at each sheet. Bonnie held onto them when they were finished.

They had no questions at all.

Under normal circumstances, they would have questions. A lot of questions.

What the hell was going on here?

Angie took a deep breath and kept going. "The third sheet is a summary of what is happening in Portland and around the world, when the first major election will be for both Portland and the United States. And so on."

"Seems very civilized like," the man said.

Again Angie pointed to her pocket. "May I?"

The man nodded and Angie pulled out an iPhone and charging cord and a paper list and offered them.

Bettie again stepped forward and took the iPhone, charging cord, and paper.

Then she stepped back beside the man.

No comment about how useless it was, nothing. More than anything Angie wanted to just turn and run, but more than likely if she did that she would be cut down from the hidden guns of the others.

"Cell towers are now working along the Interstate Five route from Portland down to Eugene and all around the Portland area," Angie said. "That's a list of numbers you can call for more information if you go down near the freeway. And your aunt's number is on there as well."

Nothing. Not one bit of comment at all.

Angie had every alarm bell in her body going off. She had to get out of there and get going now!

She smiled. "Nice chatting with all of you. I hope you decide to stop into the city when you get a chance. It's very nice."

She raised her hands and stepped backwards.

"I don't think you'll be leaving just yet," the man said, bringing his rifle up and aiming at her.

Bonnie and Bettie did the same.

Behind her, she heard a man huffing. She glanced over her shoulder to see a man pushing her bike up the road. "This is a nice ride," he said as he got over the crest of the small rise.

"What's going on here?" she asked.

"We never allow visitors to leave once they know we are here," the man said.

"We have to protect ourselves," Bettie said.

"We are so sorry," Bonnie said.

But to Angie she didn't look sorry at all. More than likely numbers of people had stumbled into this place and were buried in back somewhere, which is where she was about to end up.

Why had she ever thought she could do this job alone?

THREE

"I AM NO threat to you," Angie said. "All we wanted to do was tell you about what was happening. You are free to stay here for the rest of your lives. No one cares."

"Someone always cares," the man said.

The two women nodded. Both of them looked very pained. Clearly the year after the Event had not gone well for them.

The man pushing the bike had stopped behind her about ten steps right at the tree line. She had no doubt, without looking, that he had a gun trained on her as well.

If these people were so worried about being found, maybe Angie had one last thing to say to save her life.

"If you allow me to leave here," Angie said, "I will just cross this compound off as not interested."

"I am sure you would," the man said.

"But if you kill me, if anything happens to me, the new government will come swooping in here faster than you can ever imagine. Murder is still murder in a civilized world."

"No one knows where you are at," the man said, laughing. "You're just like those religious types who used to bang on doors back when the world was still alive. You just want us to follow you to your church so you can take our things."

"Check the bag on my bike," Angie said, staring at the man. "There are satellite images of this compound that were taken just recently. They are watching us now as I speak because they knew I was going to be here. You think I am stupid enough to walk in here alone?"

She was damn proud of herself that her voice didn't shake when she said that, even though she had been just as stupid as she claimed not to be.

The man nodded and behind Angie she could hear the other guy rummaging in her pack. He pulled out the photos of this compound and let out a small gasp. Then he let the bike drop and moved around Angie to hand the images to the man between Bonnie and Bettie.

The man looked at them and suddenly didn't seem so sure of himself.

"So go ahead and shoot me," Angie said. "But expect the helicopters and police to descend on this compound in less than two hours. But you let me go, I just cross this place off as you not being interested and you can go on with your lives for as long as you want."

"I think you are bluffing," the man said.

"Look at the photo," she said, actually bluffing her socks off. "Can you tell when it was taken? I left Portland two days ago with it. They took it for me so I would know what they were watching and so I could find this place easily. You are my third stop. They watch me closely at every stop."

The man looked at the photo, then simply tore it up and dropped it on the ground.

"We let you leave and for sure you tell everyone about us. We kill you and take the chance that you weren't being watched. I think we'll go with that second chance."

He raised his gun and at that moment all four of them just slumped to the ground. And there was a crashing beside the road and another woman slumped out of a tree and fell to the ground.

What the hell was going on?

She stood there staring at the four bodies in front of her, letting her racing heart slow just a little. She had been seconds away from being very dead.

Very, very dead.

What had happened?

At that moment, a man came walking up the road, smiling at her. "Bet you thought you were bluffing, didn't you?"

She opened her mouth to say something, then just shut it.

The guy walking toward her had a smile that lit up his face and a body that would turn any head. He looked to be about six-foot tall, with wide shoulders and short, dark hair. His skin looked smooth and tan, as if he spent a lot of time in the sun. He wore jeans, a dark green T-shirt, and had a gun on his hip in a holster that just looked like it belonged there.

"Angie, sorry we had to finally meet like this," he said, extending his hand.

She took his calm, dry hand in her sweaty hand and shook it, still stunned beyond words as to what had happened.

"I'm Lieutenant Gabby Teal, Former United States Special Forces. I've been in charge of your protection detail for the last six months."

"Holy shit," she said, almost gasping for air. "You just saved my life."

"And that's exactly why we have been watching you all along," he said, smiling. "Me and my men always went in ahead of your scheduled stop to make sure you got the protection you needed."

"Thank you," she said, not really knowing what to think other than that she was still alive and the man responsible could be a Greek God. Wearing a damn T-shirt that showed muscles no human should ever have.

"I thought you were going to talk your way out of this mess as well," he said. "You had the nut ball thinking there for a while."

She laughed. "Desperation brings on wild stories. I just didn't know any of them were true."

"Ninety-nine percent of the time," he said, "it is better to think you are alone when facing these survivors. Glad we were here for that one percent."

"Yeah," Angie said, "me, too." She was still trying to catch her breath. Near-death experiences can make you real short of breath it seemed.

"Can you help me get these people rounded up? My men have spread out to scout the area to make sure no one else is around."

"Are they dead?" Angie asked. "And what kind of weapon was that?"

"A ray guy, actually," he said, laughing "sort of along the same principle as the wave that killed us, only not fatal. Just knocks a person out for a few hours and gives them a real nasty headache."

"Good," she said, laughing.

"The fifth one fell out of a tree over here where we stunned her," he said, moving off to the right.

They each took one of the woman's arms and dragged her back to the others in the middle of the road. She was about Angie's age, around thirty, and also looked as clean and fresh as the others. But clearly the Event and this leader guy had really twisted their minds and made them into killers.

"Where is the sixth one?" she asked after they got the woman near the others.

"In the big house," he said. "We can leave her there for the pickup."

"What are you going to do with them?" she asked.

"Helicopter will take them down into the old Central America and dump them off with enough water and food to survive for a few days. It's pretty wild down there still. Perfect for their type. What they manage to do from there is their business."

She laughed. "I love that. Serves the creeps right."

He walked her back to her bike and helped her get it upright again. Her helmet must still be down near the highway.

She secured her bag on her bike and then turned to look at him. Damn, he had green eyes.

She loved green eyes.

Now she wasn't sure if her heart was still racing from almost being killed or racing because the man standing next to her was so damn good-looking.

How was it possible that the man who had saved her ass was handsome and had green eyes?

"How about from now on out we do this as a team?" she asked.

"We have been a team since you went out the first time," he said, smiling. "You just didn't know it."

"How about you and I work together then, so I know your plans and I don't go off course and change plans on you and get myself killed in some place you can't rescue my skinny ass?"

Three Seeders Universe Novels
Available at your favorite booksellers.

He laughed. "I like that a lot. So what are your plans next?"

"I'm going back to Portland to my wonderful house and my two cats, take a long, cool bath, and try to stop shaking."

He nodded, the smile still on his face.

"After that I am going to go out and have a nice dinner at a nice restaurant and a few drinks to try to bury the memory of these nut cases."

"Would you like company for dinner and a few drinks?" he asked.

"I would love that," she said. "Do you know where I live?"

She wasn't sure that she wanted to know the answer to that, but she had asked anyway.

"Not a clue," he said.

"Northwest sector of town," she said. "You ever heard of a restaurant called Danny's in the Pearl area?"

"Best chicken in all of Portland," he said, his smile lighting up an already hot and bright day.

"Six p.m.," she said, climbing on her bike and firing it up.

"Six p.m.," he said, nodding to her.

She turned her bike and headed slowly down the dirt road, not daring to look at the lieutenant behind her.

She had almost died, been rescued by the most handsome man left on the planet, and now she had a date with him.

If he had come in on a white horse it wouldn't have made it any stranger, other than the fact that horses had been killed in the Event as well.

Who knew that facing down crazy survivalists could get her a date.

It was a strange damn world, of that there was no doubt.

And she was going to enjoy every minute of still being alive, and maybe later, every inch of the body of the man who saved her.

A girl could hope.

⌇

DEAN WESLEY SMITH

A Beautiful Ghost,
A Hunk of a Cop.
Toss in a Bad Guy
Watch the Sparks Fly.

A GREAT FIRST DAY

A Ghost of a Chance Story

Eve Bryson, ghost agent, assigned to work with Deputy Cascade, superhero cop.

Cascade rolls nice guy, handsome stud, and superhero into a tight package. What could a horny ghost of a girl do?

Before Eve suggests a ghost affair, they experience a first day on the job together. She soon learns that lust sometimes takes a side seat to saving lives.

A Ghost of a Chance story that expands the universe. Don't miss this one if you enjoy the series. Or if you want to jump into the series for the first time.

A GREAT FIRST DAY
A Ghost of a Chance Story

ONE

EVE BRYSON WAS dead. Deputy McCall Cascade was alive.

They had been assigned to work together. No one said anything about sex, but a girl could hope, couldn't she? Especially when Cascade was a real superhero and more handsome than a Greek God.

For Eve, the training with the other Ghost of a Chance agents had gone great, and now she knew how to be inside another person, control that living person, teleport anywhere she wanted to go, and do a ton of other stuff that ghost agents could do.

With the help of a few other superheroes, including the famous Poker Boy and his girlfriend Patty, Eve had her own condo in the Pearl district. Patty said they were so rich they didn't know what to do with all their money, so they could use it as a tax shelter.

Patty and Sherri, two superheroes, even helped Eve furnish her condo the way she wanted it so she had her own place, with dishes, a toilet seat without a lid, and everything.

The other ghost agents found it great that she was working with a superhero as a partner.

A live superhero.

Something very different.

As one of them said, she was doing something that had never been tried before in thousands and thousands of years.

It was going to be interesting to see how it worked out.

Up until a few weeks ago, she didn't even know that any of this ghost and superhero world even existed. But she had to admit, being dead and being a ghost agent was a lot better than being alive and being with the worthless husband she had been stupid enough to marry. She didn't miss him or her old crappy job at all.

And she really didn't miss being alive in the slightest. This was much, much better.

And one of the very weird things about being dead was that the food tasted better. Everything around her seemed more alive as well, and from what one of the other ghost agents had hinted at, the sex was better too.

With other ghost agents.

But she was far, far more interested in having sex with Cascade. And he seemed to be interested in her as well. He stood six feet tall, had super-short brown hair, a chiseled chin, and a smile that could melt the paint off a freeway sign at a half-mile.

She had long brown hair, a sort of button nose that others found cute and she found sort of weird, and blue eyes, and she only came up to his chest in height. She could make him laugh and he liked that.

Since she had been inside his head, she knew he liked her, was attracted to her, wanted to be with her. They just hadn't figured out the logistics of a relationship yet between live and ghost. If she had anything to say about it, they would.

It might take time. Both of them had all the time in the world. She was dead, he was basically immortal. Worked out perfectly.

Cascade's boss in the superhero land had given him the power to see and hear her. And so all they had to do was be careful that he wasn't seen talking to himself too much, since no one else could see her.

To solve that problem, he had gotten a thin microphone that extended from an earpiece. So if someone did see him talking, they would think he was just talking into his microphone.

The only other thing they had to be careful of was the dash camera when he made stops.

On her first full day back from training with the other ghost agents, she and Cascade had figured it would be a good idea for her to just ride along with him on a standard patrol.

She liked that idea. Neither of them was sure how this "working together" was going to work out, so a standard patrol day seemed like a logical place to start.

The patrol car smelled faintly of his soap combined with a leather smell from his belt and a computer smell from the equipment between the seats. She liked this car. It had been her refuge from the rain after her car wreck the first hour she was a ghost. She had sat naked in the back seat and Cascade hadn't even known it.

When she told him later he said, "Bummer, sorry I missed that."

Now she felt comfortable in the front seat beside him, sitting in her jeans and white blouse, her hair pulled back.

He was in his full uniform, blue with dark trim, with a wide-brimmed hat just behind him on the floor between the seats so he could grab it easily.

The Portland early July weather was still only in the 80s, with bright sun warming up the afternoon. They had started their patrol at seven in the morning and since there were no cameras or microphones in the car, they chatted about her training, about the few other ghost agents she had met, and so on.

Then a half-hour into the ride, he saw a speeder in a blue Ford sedan passing cars in a no-passing area.

"There's an accident waiting to happen," she said.

"Let's see if we can stop it from happening," he said, flipping on his lights and pulling out after the speeder.

At the same time, he tapped a button on his steering wheel and on the computer screen she could see he was connected to his dispatcher.

Through a shorthand form of talking that she really needed to learn, he gave their location and what he was after and where the speeder was heading.

Eve had never been in a car chasing another car before.

It felt weird.

And exhilarating.

It would have been scary, but nothing could hurt her. So instead she worried about Cascade.

The moment the blue Ford saw Cascade's flashing lights, it signaled and pulled over, almost sliding to a stop in the gravel shoulder of the highway.

"Guy is in a hurry somewhere," Eve said.

Cascade pulled in behind him, reporting their position.

"Give me a moment to check it out," Eve said.

She went out through the door and up to the driver's side. What she saw through the driver's window shocked her for a moment.

The guy was a young man, sweating, and clearly scared, his eyes round and his breathing rushed. And slouched down in the passenger seat beside him was a very pregnant wife who was also sweating and shouting in pain. She looked to be about to pop a kid right onto the floor mat.

Eve waved for Cascade to hurry.

He jumped out of the patrol car, ran up beside Eve, took one look at the scene and said to the driver. "Stay on my bumper all the way."

"Thank you, officer," the young, soon-to-be-father said.

Cascade and Eve both ran back to the patrol car and with lights flashing, Cascade pulled out and the blue Ford did the same, staying right with Cascade as he drove and reported in what was happening, alerting the hospital to stand ready.

Six minutes later at the closest hospital, the blue Ford was met with a doctor, a couple nurses, and a stretcher. The almost-mother was rushed inside. From what Eve could tell, they made it with minutes to spare. That kid wanted to be born.

Cascade smiled at Eve as they climbed back into the cruiser. "Now that's the kind of thing I wish would happen more often."

"Nice way to start my first day on the job," Eve said.

And it was.

She felt great.

TWO

THE REST OF the morning was uneventful and they stopped for lunch at a Denny's Restaurant. Cascade kept his microphone on his head and she sat across from him so they could talk like a normal couple.

He ordered a French dip and fries, which sounded good to her as well, so when it came, she just took the ghost component of his meal.

At lunch she found out more about him, how he had gone to college, had degrees, then served four years in the Marines, seeing minor combat in the last stages of the Iraq war. Then he had gone through the police academy and discovered he was really, really good at everything to do with law enforcement.

"Is that when you were recruited to be a superhero?" Eve asked.

He nodded, finishing off his last fry. "I still don't know much about this superhero business, but I'm learning."

"So we can both learn together," she said, laughing.

"I like that idea a lot," he said, giving her that smile that made places damp that should not be damp for a ghost in a Denny's Restaurant.

They headed back out on patrol and thirty minutes later were working along a winding road that stayed next to a river and connected two of the smaller towns outside of Portland. It seemed that Deputy Sheriff Cascade's territory to patrol was very, very large. The county was underfunded and thus the sheriff's department understaffed.

As they came around a corner, Eve spotted an old white panel van tucked up in the pine trees on her side. Something about it gave her a chill and she mentioned that to Cascade.

"Let's take a look," he said. "One thing I have been learning to trust is that gut-sense about things. Seems to come from somewhere."

He reported in where they were, what he was investigating, and then pulled up the small dirt road off the pavement and parked a distance behind the van.

The van was in a small clearing where the road turned around. Sun beat down on the panel van.

Cascade started to run the plates while Eve got out to see what was happening.

As she did, a man came back down a trail with a shovel. He had on bib overalls, a dirty white T-shirt under them, and heavy boots. He looked muddy, like he had been digging a while.

She had no idea really where they were, but she had a hunch digging anything in this area was going to be illegal unless this guy owned the land, and from the looks of him, his greasy black hair and old panel van, that seemed unlikely.

And as she saw him, every alarm bell she had in her head went off. Something was very wrong with him and it took her a moment to see it.

When in training the last few weeks, she had learned to look at people's auras. Her aura was extremely bright and full of colors, but she had it contained behind a shield because she was a ghost and even ghosts had enemies, she was told.

Cascade had a very, very bright aura as well, and her aura and his seemed to match in a lot of places.

She had learned that human auras often told a good story about who the person was.

This man's aura was black and very small.

He saw the sheriff's car and she could see him hesitate, clearly trying to calm himself and keep walking toward his van as if nothing was wrong.

"Time to see what you have been up to," Eve said.

She moved toward him and just let him walk right through her.

Evil.

Pure evil.

No wonder his aura was pure black. He didn't have a redeeming feature about him.

The guy had just buried a young girl he had killed, had another at his home in a basement, and was thinking about how he was now going to have to bury a cop as well. It didn't worry him, just annoyed him.

He had no guilt, no sense of anything but that he owned the world and could do what he pleased with other people's lives.

Eve let the man walk on, then she just bent over and threw up her lunch.

Never, in all her life, had she experienced anything like that. She had no idea that people like this man even existed on the planet.

THREE

AS SHE TRIED to gather herself from the horrid thoughts of that piece of trash, behind her she heard Cascade open his car door and climb out.

Shit!

She had to do something. This guy had a large pistol stuck in his belt and was about to just gun down Cascade without a hesitation.

And Cascade was too far away to warn in any real way.

She turned and in three steps was back inside the blackness that was the guy she called human trash.

He had his hand on the revolver and was turned slightly toward his van to set down the shovel. He planned to set the shovel down, draw the revolver and kill Cascade.

But not on her watch.

Not on her first day.

Not today.

Not any damn day, actually.

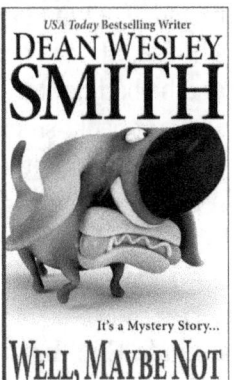

She made him freeze like something had encased him in metal.

She could feel his panic start to rise as he tried to move.

Nope, trash man. No moving for you.

The guy panicked even more hearing her voice.

Cascade must have seen her throw up, then turn and go back inside the guy. Cascade hadn't moved more than a step from his patrol car and he had his hand on his service pistol, but hadn't drawn it yet.

If she hadn't stopped this trash, Cascade would have never gotten that gun out in time to defend himself.

"Step away from the van!" Cascade shouted at the man.

The dashboard camera on the patrol car was operating, feeding a live stream back to headquarters, so she and Cascade were going to have to be careful how they handled this.

Eve decided she had had enough of the disgust in this guy's mind and with a simple tweak of a nerve that she had learned how to do in the last two weeks, she put the guy to sleep.

He fell to the ground and as he did, his hand came out holding the large gun.

Eve stepped aside, trying to use the fresh afternoon air to clear her head. They had to save that girl at the guy's house. She was in a metal box in his cellar and he had doubted she would be alive when he got back, since he planned on stopping for lunch along the way. But the trash didn't care if the girl lived or died. He actually enjoyed playing with a dead girl's body at least until they started to smell and stiffen up.

That thought almost made Eve throw up again.

She glanced back at the piece of smelly trash slumped on the ground. He would be out for about ten minutes.

Cascade instantly had his gun out and was approaching the guy as he had been trained, calling for backup as he did.

"He buried a girl up in the trees beside a couple others he killed over the last year," Eve said.

Cascade nodded slightly, looking stunned.

"We got another girl in an airtight box in his basement," Eve said. "She isn't going to last much longer."

"Shit," Cascade said, softly.

Cascade got near the guy, kicked him over, then managed to get handcuffs on the guy.

Eve moved over to Cascade and touched him so they could talk inside his head.

"I can go into that trash again, wake him, get him to confess," she said.

"You can do that?" Cascade asked without speaking.

"Never done it, but been trained how and watched it a couple times," she said, showing Cascade instantly her training. "If I get the trash to repent and tell us about the girl locked in his basement, we have a reason to get officers there quickly."

"Where is the trash's house?" Cascade asked without saying a word.

"Down off of I-5," she said. "Too far for us to make it in time to save her."

"Do it," Cascade said.

She let go of him and moved back to the piece of human garbage on the ground. Then she stepped into him again.

The blackness was intense, more than she had ever imagined it could be.

She got him to wake up and Cascade ordered the man to stay on his knees facing the patrol car and its camera.

Eve got the trash to do as Cascade ordered. Then she made the trash start bawling and sobbing like one of the girls he had killed.

"I don't want to do this anymore," the trash sobbed.

Then Eve, through the sobs, and loud enough for Cascade's microphone to pick up, got the trash to tell all about the women buried up the hill and how he wanted to save the girl in his basement.

Eve got the trash to tell Cascade his address and where the girl was exactly.

Then Eve had the guy say, "Hurry. I don't want another death on my conscious."

Eve knew this piece of human trash didn't have a conscious, but what the hell, it sounded good.

At that moment a second patrol car arrived, lights flashing, and another officer about Cascade's size and build, only with blonde hair, scrambled up beside Cascade.

Eve got the trash to repeat what he had just said.

Cascade called it in, getting officers and medical personnel rushing to the man's house.

Eve decided that this man needed even more punishment.

Jewel, one of the other ghost agents who had been a doctor before she died, had shown her how to change a person's brain in a way that caused the person extreme pain at times.

Eve had never thought she would use that, so hadn't paid a lot of attention. But she wanted more than anything to use it now. So she needed help. This guy deserved that kind of punishment.

She tweaked the nerve again and the guy pitched forward flat onto his face in the dirt.

Eve stepped out and shouted into the air, "Jewel, need some help!"

She had said to just call into the air when she needed help. And if Jewel could do what she said was possible, this was going to be fun.

FOUR

CASCADE STARTED SLIGHTLY as Jewel appeared and Eve smiled and nodded to him that it was all right.

Jewel was about Eve's age and was wearing a thin tan bikini under an open shimmering robe. Jewel could wear that bikini since she and her boyfriend exercised all the time.

Eve had forgotten to tell Cascade that she had spent the last weeks training in Las Vegas.

"Looks like the problem is pretty well covered here," Jewel said, taking a glance at the man on the ground, nodding to Cascade since Cascade could see her, then turning to Eve.

"Piece of trash there killed a bunch of women," Eve said, "just buried one up in the trees here, and has another he planned to play with when he got home, dead or alive, locked in a metal box in his basement."

"Shit," Jewel said. Then she smiled. "And you think this guy deserves a little more punishment than this fine, handsome policeman can give him?"

"I do," Eve said. "And I know you showed me how, but damned if I trust myself enough on my first day to try it."

"Come with me," Jewel said, taking Eve's hand.

They both went into the evil blackness that was the piece of trash's mind.

"Oh, one of the worst I have seen," Jewel said to Eve.

Eve could feel Jewel actually shudder.

"I hope to not see another this bad in a lot of years," Eve said.

"They are out there, sadly," Jewel said. "That's why we have the jobs we do."

Then, in the back of the man's brain, Jewel once again showed Eve how to make certain thoughts generate extreme pain.

Together, she and Jewel set the thoughts that would cause this trash pile of a human being pain. Since he hadn't cared about the pain of his victims, it was fun to have him now feel some of that pain.

They left the trash, still hand-in-hand, laughing.

Cascade watched them appear, one eyebrow up in question.

Two other cop cars had just arrived.

"We just gave this trash something to think about is all," Eve said to Cascade.

"I think you'll find it amusing," Jewel said to Cascade. "And nice meeting you. Take care of our new recruit."

He nodded and Jewel vanished.

At that moment, the piece of trash on the ground started to moan and try to struggle back to his knees.

The third cop coming up to the group said, "Great job, Cascade. They got the girl out of the box in this guy's basement and she's alive and on her way to the hospital."

Eve applauded and Cascade smiled.

"Read him his rights," Eve said, "And I'll get him to confess again."

Cascade put his gun away, got out the rights card in his shirt pocket and started reading the trash his rights as if he was a real human being.

Eve went back inside the dark, evil brain and got the guy to cry slightly again.

"Do you understand your rights?" Cascade asked the trash.

"I do," she got the guy to say.

That was on the dash camera and an officer cam one of the other officers was wearing.

"Would you like to tell us what you were doing up that hill there?" Cascade asked.

She got the trash, through tears and sobs, to make it believable, explain how he buried another body up there and where everyone he had killed was buried. And then she got him to confess to kidnapping and putting the girl in the box in his basement with the intent of killing her and having sex with her dead body."

"You are one sick piece of trash," the blonde cop said as Eve left the guy.

The two new cops on the scene moved to pull the guy up from his knees.

"Ask him if he enjoyed making love to the girls," Eve said to Cascade, smiling.

Cascade did and the piece of trash started to smile. Then the trash got this horrid look and screamed in agony and went to the ground, peeing himself as he did.

"Oh, great," one of the cops said.

The two cops yanked him back to his feet and started to drag him toward their cars.

The trash just kept screaming.

Eve went over to Cascade and put her hand on his shoulder.

"What did you and that other ghost Jewel do to the human trash?" Cascade asked without saying anything out loud.

"We just rewired his brain a slight bit is all," Eve said, laughing. "Now when he thinks about sex with anyone, boy or girl, young or old, it will feel like someone has kicked him in the groin really hard."

"You didn't?" he thought at her, but she could tell it was everything he could do to not burst out laughing.

"Other ghosts have done this to perverts and killers like this one," Eve told him. "So many times in fact, the problem is starting to get known in the medical community."

"I think I love this job," Cascade said.

"As soon as those guy's memories fade," Eve said, "I will as well."

FIVE

"MEMORIES ALMOST FADED?" Cascade asked her as the two of them sat in his living room, facing each other, sipping on a wonderful white wine. He had cooked them both a fantastic dinner of stuffed sage hen and steamed vegetables. Best meal she remembered tasting in a long time.

She said she felt bad that she couldn't cook for him but he could cook for her, since she could eat the ghost part of his meal. That was when she discovered that he loved to cook, had thought of being a chef instead of a cop after the Marines. So the fact that he could cook something for himself and have two people enjoy it was wonderful to him.

This handsome superhero really was too good to be true.

"Memories from the trash are gone," she said, smiling at him. "One of the nice things about being a ghost, the memories of people we brush through or are inside of don't stick with us for very long."

He raised his glass. "To a good first day, partner. Thanks for saving my life."

"I think that's what partners are for," she said.

After that they watched a movie and both of them fell asleep on the couch together, her inside him.

It felt wonderful to sleep with him like that. Natural.

He woke up first and stirred her and she agreed she would see him bright and early in the morning for their second day.

He wanted her to stay and she wanted to stay. But they would have time to talk about that soon enough.

Days of time riding around in a patrol car, actually.

She jumped to her condo, which actually felt empty.

She should be staying with him, making love to him.

Or at least sleeping in his arms as they had done on the couch.

She was a ghost, he was a superhero. Somehow, someone, somewhere, would know what she and Cascade could do to take the relationship to the next level.

They both wanted to.

She took a quick shower, then crawled into her wonderful bed, thinking about him.

He was handsome and he could cook and he liked her.

And today they had saved a life and helped a child be born safely.

Pretty damn fine first day together.

She fell asleep thinking of his wonderful smile.

And she was pretty sure she had a smile on her face as well.

~

Duster Kendal lost an Idaho mining town called Grapevine Springs. In 2020 he knew the town, spent time there. In 1901 the valley sat empty.

The town never existed. Not possible.

Duster needed to get back to the year 2020 to solve the mystery of the lost mining town.

A standalone story that introduces a new mining town and new characters into the Thunder Mountain world of westerns and time travel.

THE PROBLEM OF GRAPEVINE SPRINGS
A Thunder Mountain Story

ONE

DUSTER KENDAL SAT high in his saddle, turning slowly in all directions, staring at the surrounding small valley in the warm afternoon sun. The hills were pine covered, the valley floor itself fairly wide, with a gentle fall from north to south that allowed Grapevine Creek to meander back and forth from one side of the valley to the other, forming great stream banks under grass and weeds for trout to hide.

The air had a hot-pine smell and only a very faint breeze even rustled the brush under the trees.

This was the location, he was sure of it.

He wore his normal brown cowboy hat, his long oilcloth slicker, a light shirt and jeans. At six feet tall and with the long, flowing coat, he made an imposing figure in the saddle.

He finally rode slowly over to a stand of tall pine jutting off a ridgeline and into the valley floor, working his way through the grass. The trees would give him shade, a place to camp, and time to figure out what was happening.

He dismounted, allowing his horse Sandy to graze close by while he took his canteen and a map from his saddlebag. He had printed the map before he left 2020 to come back to 1901. It looked like an old map of 1900, only with far more detail than most maps of the time.

It had taken him eight years to finally get to this remote valley north of the Salmon River in Idaho, even though it had been the stated reason for his trip back. He had spent the first years helping once again to build the big log Monumental Lodge. He loved the two years building that lodge and he loved more having it always there to stay at.

Then after building the lodge, he had gone down to Denver to play some poker for a couple years. But now he was back in Idaho, on a mission that had puzzled him and others for years, both here in the past and in the future.

The mission: To find Grapevine Springs, the mining town.

He again studied the steep-walled valley as he took a drink from his canteen.

Nothing here but a remote valley.

Nothing.

At this point in history, this town should be winding its mining days down, but at least five saloons and two thousand people should be in this area right now, on June 27th, 1909.

There were no trails in here, let alone a wagon road, and as far as he could tell, the entire area hadn't even had anyone go through it besides Native Americans, let alone been settled by miners.

But it was supposed to have been.

Grapevine Springs was a very real town in 2020. A former mining town turned tourist and ski town. The tall hill across from him in the winters was covered with snowboarders and skiers. In 2020 he had stood in this very spot, actually, on the deck of a condo, watching the skiers on the hill across the valley.

The history of this town was well documented in a museum in the town's center, plus in the Idaho Historical Society.

Supposedly a married couple named Watts, prospecting out of the Thunder Mountain region, had stumbled upon color in pans in Grapevine Creek around 1901. They and a dozen silent partners out of Boise had managed to get claims in on most of the ground in this valley and had built Grapevine Springs, the town, selling off parcels of land to stores and saloons and other businesses.

At one point, Grapevine Springs had bragged that it had over ten thousand people in it working dozens of mines up and down the valley. That had been before the gold died down and the town receded back to almost a ghost town with only a few winter residents and a couple hundred landowners coming in during the summer.

In 2002, a group of investors, looking to build a major ski area destination resort like Sun Valley, visited the ghost town of Grapevine Springs. Three years later the resort opened and it grew every year since into a major tourist attraction for the State of Idaho.

But in all his years living in the past, beyond ten thousand years now from what his wife Bonnie told him, almost all of it in parts of Idaho, he had never heard of Grapevine Springs as a mining town.

In fact, at one point or another, he had been the town sheriff or marshal for most major towns in the west.

Tough to be the marshal of a town that flat didn't exist in this timeline. Or any of the other thousand timelines he had visited.

Someone, for some reason, had planted the history of Grapevine Springs in historical records.

So it actually was a real ghost town, because in the past it had never existed.

At least not in this past.

TWO

DUSTER SPENT A week exploring the wonderful, hidden valley. He caught large rainbow trout from the stream and ate them for both lunch and dinner. He never got tired of fresh rainbow trout cooked in butter so that the meat fell off the bones.

And on the third day he decided to do a little gold panning himself.

Amazing how easy it was to pull color on a pan.

He hit ten different areas of the stream for a mile upstream and a couple miles downstream, finding gold every time.

A lot of it.

There was no doubt there were some rich veins in this valley somewhere.

This area really should have been found, and how it hadn't been, he had no idea. More than likely the area was just far too remote.

So after a week of camping in the Grapevine Valley, he headed back out. It was no wonder the valley had become such a sensation in the future, it had a wonderful feel about it.

It took him a good two weeks to make his way to the Monumental Lodge, and he stayed there until just before the first snowfall in late September before heading back to Boise and the Historical Institute.

The Historical Institute had been started by him and Bonnie and twelve others who knew about timeline jumping to help historians in their research.

Most of the historians working there at the Institute knew nothing about being able to actually jump into the past of an almost identical timeline to do hands-on research.

And since each jump into another timeline only lasted two minutes and fifteen seconds, a person could stay in that other timeline, live a full life, even die, and find themselves having only a few minutes pass in their real life.

That was how he and Bonnie had lived so long.

Twenty-two others now knew about the massive hidden caverns under the main Institute building and had jumped back into the past of another timeline at different points. He and Bonnie and the other twelve founders of the Institute were very selective in who they chose.

When he finally reached Boise in late September, the year was 1910. He and others from 2020 had gone back into the past to 1880 and built this Institute so that through all periods of time, they would have a place as a base.

The Institute looked like a classic Victorian-style mansion on a bluff over-looking the Boise River. They had also built two other mansions on either side of the main one. Those housed various parts of the Institute business.

He got his horse settled in the stable behind the main mansion, patted her a goodbye, and went in through a hidden door in the stable that took him directly to the caverns under the mansion.

He quickly dropped off the gold he had panned in the regular safe, left his saddle-bags in the preparation cavern, and with only the map from the future in his hand, jumped back to 2020 by unplugging a wire from a machine he and Bonnie had invented.

The machine was simple. It was hooked to a crystal that looked like a glowing quartz crystal. The machine allowed a person touching it to step into the past of the timeline held in that crystal.

Every time a decision was made, a new timeline was formed. An infinite number of timelines for almost all major decisions.

By Duster simply being in the past of that timeline, he had caused millions of new timelines to be formed in the Nexus, the place where all energy, matter, and time combine into gigantic caverns full of crystals, each crystal holding a unique timeline.

A person could go back and alter a past, just not their own past. Only the past in another timeline.

The thousands of crystals brought to the Institute in Boise from the Nexus were all timelines virtually identical to their own. And every year or so 2020 time, all the crystals that had been used were returned to the Nexus and new ones brought out to replace them.

Now, by removing that simple wire, he had returned to 2020. June 7th, actually.

He dropped the map off on a table in the massive preparation cavern and went out into what they all called The Living Room.

He knew that Bonnie and Dawn would be there, since from this time he had only been gone the ten minutes it took him to prepare, the slightly over two minutes to live the nine years in the past, and the five minutes to walk back to the Living Room area of the cavern under the mansion.

Bonnie and Dawn were both sitting at a long kitchen counter, talking. A fire was

burning lightly in the huge stone fireplace that dominated the far wall, and no one was using the dozen couches and chair arrangements that filled the area between the fireplace and the kitchen with its long, granite-topped counter.

Bonnie and Dawn both glanced up at him and Bonnie smiled.

"Any luck?" Dawn asked. She was shorter than Bonnie, but also had long brown hair like Bonnie. She and her husband Madison had been the first two Bonnie and Duster had taken back into the past with them.

And Dawn and Madison always stayed and ran the Monumental Lodge every time they built it in 1902. In fact, he had just said goodbye to Dawn and Madison when he left the lodge in the past.

Sometimes jumping through time into varied timelines got complicated like that.

Damn he had missed Bonnie, her wonderful smile, her beautiful brown hair, and those eyes that kept him intrigued all the time. Even after thousands of years together, he was still madly in love with her.

And he knew that to her, he had only been gone twenty minutes or so. To him, he hadn't seen her in years.

He walked over and kissed her, then pointed to the showers. "It was a long ride from the lodge. I'll take a shower and tell you all about what I found."

"Good plan," Bonnie said, smiling and pretending to wave her hand at his smell.

He laughed and turned away.

"How many years?" she asked.

"Nine," he said without turning around.

Again he heard her wonderful laugh.

"Denver poker games good?" she asked.

"Wonderful," he said. "Just wonderful."

THREE

AFTER HIS SHOWER, Duster had told them about his trip, mostly focusing on the Grapevine Valley and how absolutely nothing was there.

Nothing.

That had gotten both Dawn and Bonnie even more interested, especially since Bonnie had gone with him to the condo at the Grapevine Springs Resort and they had really enjoyed it.

"I have some contacts at the Idaho Historical Society," Dawn had said. "I'll get them and two of our researchers upstairs working on this and bring what I find to our meeting next week at the lodge. We should be able to find out exactly where and when the information was planted. And maybe who did it."

Now, a week later, Duster and Bonnie had flown into the Monumental Lodge by helicopter from Boise. The flight had been stunning since the day was warm and calm and the sky a bright blue over the rugged pine-covered mountains.

Duster wasn't so much excited about the meeting, but at this point he was more interested in what Dawn and her researcher friends had found out about the fake history of Grapevine Springs.

Every few months, all of the fourteen founders got together at the Institute to talk about who to accept into the research area of the Institute and who might be ready to be told about the timeline travel part. All it took was one founder to say no and a candidate was rejected.

But before that larger meeting, Bonnie and Duster and Dawn and Madison had a private meeting about the candidates with the head of the Institute and another founder, Jesse Parks. It wasn't a secret meeting, just what Duster called a "make sure" meeting. Make sure that all five of them were on the same page going into the larger meeting.

Duster loved the feeling of the lodge. He and Bonnie, along with Dawn and Madison owned the massive log structure that sat high in a saddle overlooking the Monumental Creek drainage. One mountain to the south of the lodge was called Thunder Mountain, the mountain that gave the entire region its name.

The entire second floor was only for founders, and Bonnie and Duster had their own room that no one but them had slept in for over a hundred years.

Dawn and Madison also had a suite in the back where in various timelines they had raised children. Duster didn't want to know how many children they had raised here. He was actually afraid to ask.

The massive polished logs and the 1900s furniture had been kept exactly as it was when built all those years ago. That locked-in-time charm was one of the reasons that made getting a room in the Monumental Lodge one of the most sought-after reservations on the planet.

The fact that only ten rooms were ever rented and the food was top-flight didn't hurt the demand either.

As Bonnie and Duster arrived, a dozen or so guests were sitting on the massive deck staring out at the view over most of the central wilderness area of Idaho. To say that view was spectacular would be a giant understatement. When you can see a hundred miles over some of the most rugged mountains in the world, on a warm spring day like today it was just hard to breathe when looking at the beauty of it all.

The first time he had stood on this saddle between the two tall peaks and looked out at the view, he knew it had to have a lodge here. And he had been right. They had built it in a hundred different timelines so far. And he never tired of building it again.

And always the exact same way with the exact same floor plan and the exact same furniture. There were some things in history that just shouldn't be messed with in any timeline and the Monumental Lodge was one of those things.

Bonnie and Duster put their overnight bags into their room, then headed down to the private meeting room off the main dining room.

Jesse and Dawn were already there, talking at a ten-person wooden table in the middle of the room. The table was covered by a cloth that looked like it was straight out of 1900 and most likely was. Both had iced teas from a pitcher on a sideboard area.

Duster poured himself and Bonnie glasses of tea and sat down next to Dawn.

Jesse was the director of the Institute, the person who ran the entire thing. He was about Duster's real-world age of mid-thirties and was about the same height as Duster's six feet.

Before Jesse had ended up meeting his wife Kerri, a historian and writer, and learning about traveling into timeline pasts, Bonnie and Duster had often hired him and his private investigative firm to find out about candidates. He still did that for the institute, as well as run everything.

He and his firm dug into a person's history while his wife Kerri dug into the candidate's research and work ethic. Between the two of them and how strict they were, it was amazing any candidate got through to even be considered. But Duster liked that.

"Any luck on the Grapevine Springs strangeness?" Duster asked Dawn as he and Bonnie got settled at the table.

"None," she said. "Whoever made up that history and planted it, did a perfect job of it. None of us can find a seam anywhere to pick at."

"Damn that's weird," Duster said. "But someone had to have made it all up, since I camped for a week in that valley in the year the town should have been winding down and there was nothing at all there. Nothing."

"What town?" Jesse asked.

"You know the ski resort called Grapevine Springs Resort?" Dawn asked.

"The one up north of here a hundred miles or so?"

"That's it," Dawn said. "It has a history of once being a booming mining town."

"But there is no town there in 1909," Duster said. "No signs a town was ever there."

"So we think the ski resort owners forged the entire history and planted it to give some depth and history to their resort," Bonnie said.

"It wouldn't be the first time," Jesse said, nodding.

"We're convinced that's what happened," Dawn said. "They would have no idea we could go back and actually check on their fake history."

"We're just wondering how they did it," Duster said.

"Driving me crazy," Dawn said. "And I got two history grad students at the University almost in tears trying to find where all the information was planted."

"Oh, you are mean," Bonnie said, laughing.

"I didn't tell them their grade would depend on it," Dawn said, smiling.

"But you might have hinted," Jesse said, shaking his head and smiling.

"I might have," Dawn said, looking sheepish.

They all laughed and the conversation continued until Madison joined them after taking care of a few guests. Then the five of them had a wonderful meal of spring trout, pan-fried better than Duster could have done over a campfire.

Finally, after a wonderful sorbet for dessert, the dishes were cleared, coffee served, and the five of them got down to the meeting.

"We had thirty-five applications for funding this last three months," Jesse said. "Ten of the straight funding for projects Kerri and I just approved."

He handed to each of them a sheet with a two-line description of the funded projects and the amounts.

Duster only glanced at it. The Institute had more money than any one place should ever have, and was constantly generating more from all the investments around the world. They could have given a thousand times more away than those requests and not even have it be noticed in the petty cash fund.

But Duster knew that to remain an Institute that seemed aboveboard and well-funded, Jesse and his people had to do all this stuff and keep the levels within reason. Duster was just glad they had someone in that position he trusted to do it.

"We turned down another twenty projects," Jesse said, "from people who just wanted the money and had no capability of even following through on the research."

"So that leaves five," Bonnie said, nodding.

Jesse nodded. "All research requests for the person to come to the Institute and research specific historical projects for varying amounts of time."

Duster nodded. They had almost sixty researchers at any point working in the various libraries and buildings in Boise that the Institute owned. And if a person was accepted to the Institute, all expenses were paid, including food, plus a large salary, and no claim was made against the researchers' final product.

That kind of package was why so many quality researchers applied to the Institute. And it also allowed Jesse and everyone to observe them over months or a year to see if they might be candidates for learning about the timeline jumping that went on under the Institute.

Historical research always tended to be so much better when a person could go back into another timeline and actually see the place they were researching.

"Any good ones?" Bonnie asked.

"Actually," Jesse said, "I think all five are good. One wants to do a definitive book on those who fought at the Alamo, not only who they were, but their families and their histories that took them to that place."

"Nifty," Dawn said.

Jesse handed a folder full of information about that person to Bonnie. She glanced at it and handed it to Duster.

Duster also just glanced at it and handed it to Dawn. He knew later tonight that he and Bonnie would go over each candidate's application. All of them would, and if there were any questions, they would talk it out at breakfast before flying back to Boise for the larger meeting.

"Two of the candidates are a couple working together on a project," Jesse said. "They want to take an old mining town population and backtrack each inhabitant's history as much as possible. And do various books on the reasons why certain people and families ended up in these old boom towns."

"That's kind of taking my research and expanding it," Dawn said, nodding. "I like that."

"They quoted your books a great deal in their presentation," Jesse said, nodding. "They don't know you are involved with the Institute, but are clearly major fans of your books."

"I'm looking forward to meeting them," Dawn said, smiling.

Jesse handed the folder to Bonnie, who glanced at it and then handed it to Duster.

He was about to pass the folder along when a name caught his attention.

He looked up at Jesse. "The guy's name is Stephen Watts?"

"You are kidding me?" Dawn asked. "What's his wife's name?"

"They won't be married for another two weeks," Jesse said.

"Her name is Connie," Duster said, studying the file and shaking his head.

Dawn just laughed while Jesse, Bonnie, and Madison all looked puzzled.

Duster handed the file to Dawn.

"It seems," Duster said, "that we approve these two all the way to the caverns."

"Or they will be," Dawn said, still laughing as she studied the file.

"Why do you say that?" Jesse asked.

"Because they build Grapevine Springs," Duster said. "The reason it wasn't there yet in the past is because they hadn't built it in the past yet."

"Talk about a perfect research project," Dawn said. "Start your own mining boom town and then study all the people in it."

"Lost me," Jesse said.

"Just like when we come back to this ridge in 1900 in various timelines," Dawn said, "and there is no lodge. We haven't built it yet."

"Exactly," Duster said. "We build it in the past of a lot of timelines so that it sits here in this one now."

Jesse nodded, starting to understand. "So at some point we tell these two about the caverns and time travel and they go back and start Grapevine Springs."

"Sure seems that way," Dawn said. "No wonder we couldn't find where the history was planted. It wasn't."

"And how much you want to bet," Duster said, "that we are the secret investors from Boise who help them build that mining town?"

"No bet," Dawn said. "But I better call off my researchers before they discover that we are the investors."

"So in some other timeline," Bonnie said, "we approve these two for the caverns and timeline travel and they build that town in this timeline."

"And in a bunch of timelines chances arc we don't approve them," Duster said.

"And they don't build it. Our timeline, this timeline, just happens to be one of the lucky ones."

"So seems to be a chicken and egg issue," Jesse said. "We know we approve them in some timelines because they build the town."

"So are we going to approve them in this timeline because we know that we do in other timelines?" Duster asked, smiling at Jesse. He sometimes loved poking at his good friend when it came to puzzling time issues.

"That seems to be the question," Jesse said.

"Are they good candidates?" Bonnie asked, not letting Duster say anything more to poke Jesse.

She knew him far too well.

"Great ones," Jesse said.

"They we approve them for regular research," Bonnie said, "and watch them as we watch any of the others until we are satisfied they are ready for the caverns and timeline travel."

"Exactly," Duster said. "It won't matter if we show them the caverns tomorrow or ten years from tomorrow. They

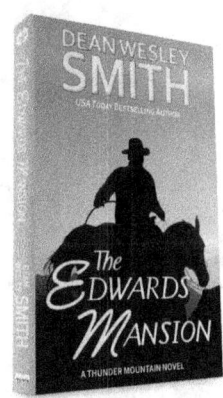
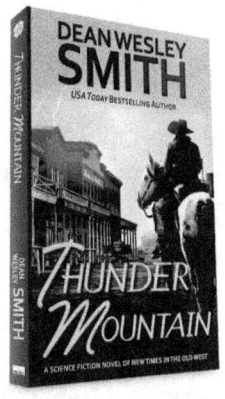

can jump back from any point and build that town."

Everyone at the table nodded.

"But to be honest," Dawn said, "I want to approve them as soon as we are sure about them."

"Why?" Duster asked, wondering why she was so excited. Normally Dawn was one of the more conservative ones in the founders.

"Because I love the idea of being with a town you help start from the beginning all the way through its natural life cycle," she said.

"That is kind of cool," Madison said.

"But mostly it's clear I was there as well," Dawn said. "And so were all of you."

She reached into the file she had brought about the research on Grapevine Springs and pulled out an old picture.

She handed it to Duster, who just laughed. Damn this was fun.

There, standing on a sidewalk in front of a general store was Dawn, square in focus, looking at something in a wagon. The picture was dated 1907.

And in the background, standing in a small group, were Madison, Jesse, and Bonnie. And Duster was standing with his back to the camera, but with his coat and hat, it was clear it was him.

"You know you have a good project presentation," Duster said, smiling and handing the picture to Bonnie, "When you have photographs proving it was already approved."

"Boy, got that right," Bonnie said, laughing as she looked at the picture of herself taken well over a hundred years before.

"It seems the mystery of Grapevine Springs has been solved," Dawn said.

Duster nodded. He liked that. He had hated the idea that history could be cheated by simply being planted for the sake of money. That had bothered him more than he wanted to admit.

To him, history was everything. He loved history, he loved supporting the research into history. He loved the researchers who worked to get history correct, no matter how politically wrong or inconvenient that might be.

And more than anything, he loved living in the history.

Even after thousands of years of living in the past, it just never got old.

Now Available
from all your favorite booksellers
in trade paper and electronic editions.

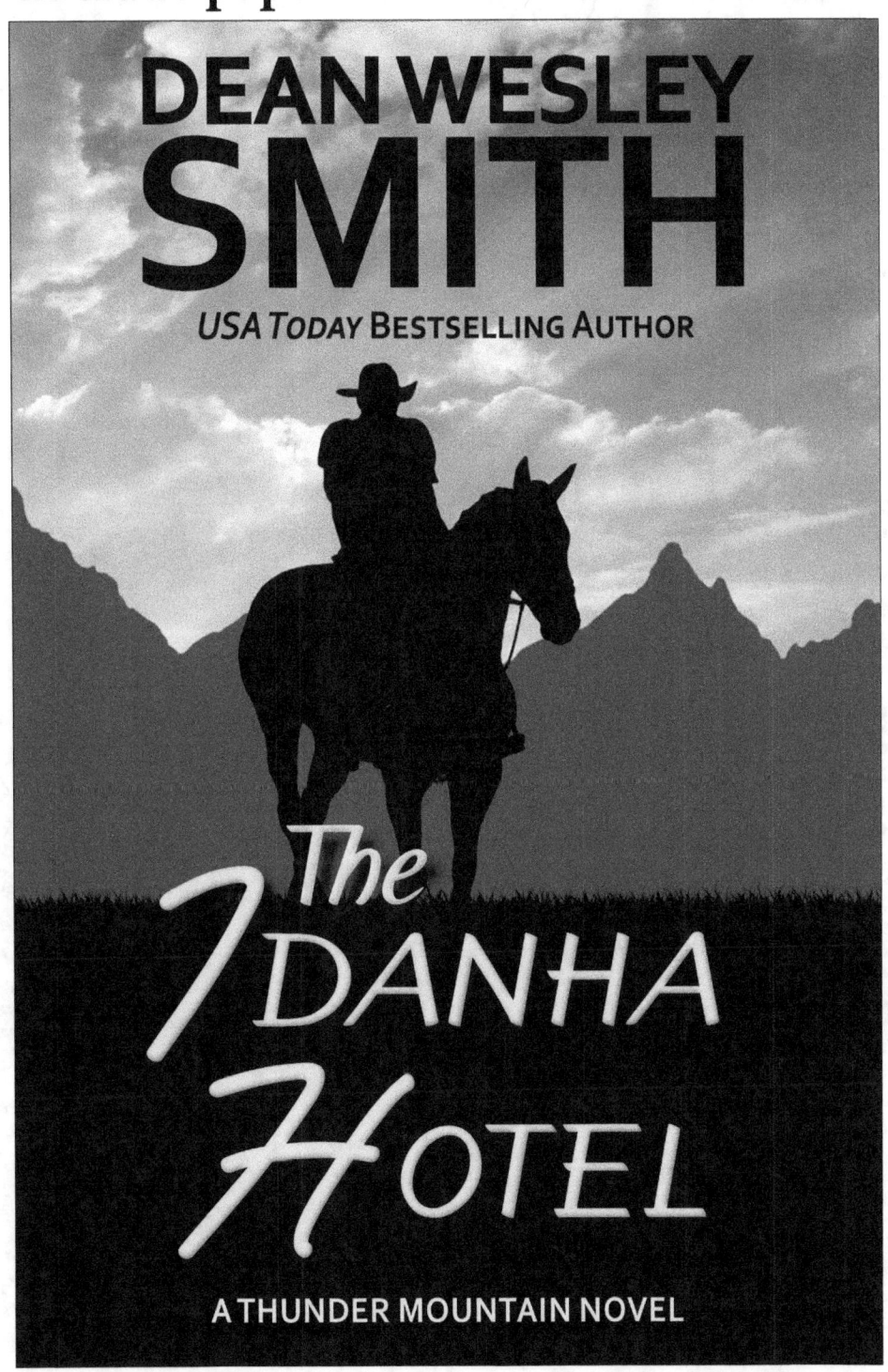

DEAN WESLEY
SMITH
USA *Today* BESTSELLING AUTHOR

The
Idanha
Hotel

A THUNDER MOUNTAIN NOVEL

DEAN WESLEY SMITH

LAYING THE MUSIC TO REST

A former college professor turned bartender, Doc finds himself trying to save his friends from a ghost under a lake in the wilderness of Idaho.

From diving into a ghost town buried under a lake to trying to stay alive on the sinking deck of the Titanic, this time-travel science fiction novel reads like a roller-coaster ride with all the twists and turns.

First published in paperback in 1989 from Warner Questar Books, Dean Wesley Smith's first published novel gives a lot of hints of his future series and his bestselling career spanning over a hundred and fifty novels.

Published here in its original form, without any changes, just as Dean wrote it almost thirty years ago.

LAYING THE MUSIC TO REST
Part 5

CHAPTER EIGHT

Monumental Lodge
June 29, 1990

"I THINK YOU'VE finally gone and lost it, old buddy," Fred said. It was almost noon and he was leaning against a handmade wooden dresser in my room, watching me pack what clothes I could into the bottom part of a large backpack.

"You may be right about that one," I said.

"So then what's the point?"

I shrugged without looking up. "Might as well finish what I came up here for."

"Damn it, Doc. You and I both know that's not it. You came up here so I wouldn't kill myself making a stupid dive into a lake. Not to go using some strange mirror to jump you to God only knows where."

"I know." In the lifetime I had been with Fred, I had seen a lot of worry cross his face. Right now it wasn't crossing, it was lodged tight, right out in the open.

"Look on it as an adventure," I said. "Besides, if Susan is right—"

"And if she's wrong?"

"Then look on it as an adventure." I didn't want to think about the obvious possibility that she was wrong. And maybe dead. "What the hell. We've done crazy things before. Like the dive into that lake out there. Remember?"

"That was crazy," Fred said. "This is just plain suicidal."

"You don't know that. And neither do I. But at least give me my choice of going out the way I like. All right? Hasn't that been an understood agreement between us all these years? As long as we went out doing something we wanted to do, everything would be fine. No bad feelings and all that. Well, I want to do this. And see, I'm smiling."

I gave him one of the biggest, phoniest grins I could and he laughed and shook his head.

"Besides, Susan seemed to know what she was doing," I said. "And it didn't look like suicide to me. Admit it. You're jealous. You really want to go along, but know Constance would kill you if you even suggested it. Right?"

Again, he laughed. "Not really. I'm more worried about you."

"Okay for you to worry if you want. But the question is, are you going to help? If so, see how Constance is coming with the food."

Fred shook his head. "I ever tell you that you're impossible to reason with?"

"I learned it all from you."

"I'll check on the food." He turned and went back out the door and I listened as he plodded down the stairs.

He knew I was as worried and afraid as he was. It had been a long night of almost no sleep. I'd thought it through over and over and had kept coming back to the same conclusion. I wanted to see what was on the other side of that mirror. And even more than that, I wanted desperately to not have to go back to that bar and all those nights alone in that house. That was truly the bottom line.

Yesterday, when Susan disappeared out of that chair, I knew that I had found my escape. Not just the pretend escape from a boring classroom to a boring bar. Susan proved her story by proving the mirror was what she said it was. There was a possible new start where she had gone and my little voice was yelling for me to not miss the opportunity. In other words, escape. Run like hell. Jump the wall. Do all those other clichés that come up when a person is trying to rationalize a change in his life. Most people go through life fearing change, hanging by their fingernails to what they know, afraid of the dark, evil "what if" around the corner. I had always scorned those types of people. Yet, in many ways I had done the same thing. Now, finally, I'd found a true adventure. A true chance at change.

I was scared flat silly.

I tucked the last of the clothes into the pack and pulled the zipper tight. Then I swung it up on my shoulder and took one more quick look around the room. There was nothing more I needed here, or for that matter, back in Boise. For some reason, that thought made me feel very light.

I headed down the stairs. Through the front window, I could see that the sun had begun to fill the bottom of the valley in its losing battle to warm the waters of the small lake.

Constance brought the small daypack full of food out of the kitchen and set it on the table beside the other provisions as I leaned the big pack against the wall. She looked up at me. She had the same lines of worry etched in her face that Fred had in his. Of course, if the situation were reversed, I would look the same. And I would be protesting just as much. I also hoped that if they insisted, I would do everything in my power to help. That's the way it had always been between us.

Fred, Steven, and I worked at packing everything and making contingency plans as Constance fixed a huge lunch. Since we had no idea exactly where I was going, we packed every survival type of item the four of us could think of, from boxes of matches to toilet paper. There were flints, a mirror, knives, and a string saw. The food Constance packed would last me almost two weeks if I was careful. I also had a medical kit far in excess of what a normal hiker would carry, plus a compass and world map.

After a huge lunch, forced down me by Constance with the rationale, "You never know when you're going to get a solid meal again," Fred and I rechecked the list we had made the night before to make sure everything was included. The pack weighed out at one hundred and eighty-six pounds, sleeping bag, rifle, and all. If I ended up someplace where I had to carry that sucker farther than a few hundred yards, I would be in trouble. Hell, for all I knew, I might end up in an apartment on Broadway. Or maybe in a cave in Africa. Or in a jungle. But, as Fred said, if I was stupid enough to do this, the least I could do was be prepared for almost anything. I could always ditch the stuff I didn't need.

Finally, everything was ready and I had given my last hugs to Constance and Fred. Both Fred and Steven helped me put the pack on. Damned if I knew how, short of falling down, I was going to get it off by myself. I mentioned that to Fred but he didn't think it at all funny.

With the pack, I sat down on the edge of the coffee table and picked up the mirror. "I don't know what to suggest you do with this," I said. "Just make sure you keep it safe. After Susan's comment, there might be others after it. All right?"

Constance had tears in her eyes, but she nodded.

"But do try to keep it out in the open," I added. "I might come back through it real soon.

"You know," Fred said, "I wish you weren't doing this. I mean—"

"Don't," I said. "My stomach is already so damn tight I can hardly breathe. On second thought, maybe it's this pack." I tried adjusting the pack for the show of it, but didn't get much of a smile from the three solemn faces staring at me. "All right, it's not the pack. I'm scared to death. Now, are you satisfied?"

"Not until you change your mind," Fred said.

I shook my head. "Just keep the home fires burning. I'll be all right. And if not, you know where my will is. Just don't give my stuff away too soon."

"Damn it, Doc," Constance said. "Don't—"

I held up my hand for her to stop. "Just kidding. Tell Angie I'll be back before the students return from summer break. And tell her to hire someone to water the damn plants. She always forgets."

Fred nodded.

"If possible, I'll try to get some sort of signal back to you. Maybe through the ghost or something. Damned if I know how."

"I'm sure she'll be around," Steven said.

Again, Fred nodded but didn't say anything.

I picked up the mirror and looked in it. For a brief second, my own image surprised me. I had my navy stocking cap pulled down tight and my parka wrapped around Fred's rifle and strapped across the top of the sleeping bag behind my head.

I looked into the mirror for a moment, then over at Fred. He did not look happy. He looked like any moment he was going to jump forward and pull the mirror from my hands. I winked at him.

I was so scared I could hardly hold the mirror steady enough to look in it. What the hell was I doing? I looked over at Fred and then back at my own image in the shaking mirror. My nerve was fading fast. This was like jumping off a cliff. It was either now or never.

I had started to run my hands along the outside of the mirror, copying what Susan had done, when movement caught my eye.

"Constance!" Fred shouted. "Move!"

Within a foot of where Constance was standing, the air was shimmering. Constance jumped quickly aside as Gretchen took form, facing me. Constance and Fred both moved around to give her room. The ghost stood staring at me. Or more likely at the mirror.

"I'm going to see if I can find Alex," I said after a long moment of silence. The ghost made no motion that she had heard me. Then, as quickly as she had come, she faded.

I glanced around at Steven. He was still standing there with his eyes clear, watching intently.

"I didn't catch a thing," he said.

No one said another word and so finally, I looked into the mirror at my own worry-lined face. If I didn't do it soon, I would never have the courage again.

I took a deep breath to try to calm my shaking hands and sick stomach. Then I looked myself right in the eye and ran my hand clockwise around the smooth ivory frame.

Quickly, I laid the mirror facedown on the coffee table beside me.

For a moment, I thought nothing was going to happen. I was about to reach for the mirror and try again, when I noticed the room seemed to be glowing.

I glanced over at Fred and then up at Constance. They were shimmering, as if I were looking at them through a layer of slightly moving clear water.

"Doc!" I heard Constance shout, but her voice sounded very far away.

"I'll be back," I tried to shout at them. But I think it was too late.

I was in complete blackness.

I had no feeling. Nothing.

No up. No down. No weight. No smell.

Nothing.

My eyes were open and I couldn't see a thing.

CHAPTER NINE

Boat Deck
First Cycle
April 14, 1912

THE BLACKNESS FADED quickly, with the light coming back like someone was turning up a dimmer switch.

I was now standing. I couldn't remember straightening my legs, but I ended up that way without a bump or the slightest feeling of movement. As the blackness faded, my weight and the heavy feel of the pack returned.

I was outside, on the deck of a ship, facing over a gray-blue ocean into a setting sun that stabbed streamers of red across the sky. It had been near noon when I left. It was obviously much later wherever I was now.

I took a deep breath and tried to calm down. My heart raced like it was going to explode. That was almost comforting. At least I wasn't dead. Or it didn't feel like I was.

I seemed to be on the top deck of a very large ship. A biting cold wind cut at my face. I could smell the salt in the air as the bow of the ship plowed through the ocean swells, sending huge walls of water crashing off to each side and a fine mist of spray back over the lower decks.

I started to do a quick turn to look around and ended up catching myself on the rail. The damn pack almost tipped me off into the water. The stupid thing weighed a ton.

Slowly, so as not to pull a muscle, I knelt down and eased the pack off onto the deck. Then I unwrapped my coat from the rifle and put it on. The wind was cold and seemed to be getting more so with every passing second. That would figure. I couldn't jump to someplace warm with beaches and lots of sun. No sir. It had to be cold.

I took a pair of pants out of the bottom zipper of the pack, wrapped the rifle in them so it couldn't be seen, and secured it back to the top of the pack frame.

Then I stood and glanced around. No one seemed to be paying me any mind at all. Toward the stern of the ship, a dozen passengers in heavy, old-style coats walked the deck or stood by the rails between the large wooden lifeboats that hung from crane-like arms along the side. The walking passengers turned back at a rope barrier strung across the deck from a lifeboat to a window frame. It seemed that I had landed in an off-limits section of the ship. Maybe this was the normal landing area for people coming through the mirror.

Ocean on the right as I faced the bow meant I was on the starboard side of the ship. On my left seemed to be the bridge of the ship. Seven men in blue, formal-looking uniforms were working. Three stood at panels. Another slowly moved a large wheel while staring out over the rolling sea.

The bow of the ship had to be a good two hundred feet from where I stood. Behind me, the ship seemed to stretch into the distance. It was one of the biggest ships I had ever seen. Much bigger than any of the transport ships I had been on. I had prepared myself for ending up in a lot of different places. But not once did I think it would be a ship, especially a passenger liner already at sea.

I took another deep breath and tried to force myself to relax enough to think straight. With any luck, Susan was somewhere on the ship, assuming that the mirror had sent me to the same place it had her. I didn't want to think about the chances that it hadn't. I had decided to go through the mirror with the assumption that it would send me to the same place and now it was far too late to start questioning that belief. Susan was here. Wherever here was.

I dragged the pack across the deck and leaned it against the bulkhead, then zipped up my coat and went back over to the rail. The water was a good eighty feet below me. As far as I could see in the quickly fading light, there was nothing but rolling ocean. No other ships or any sign of land. Absolutely no telling where I could be.

I took a few more breaths of deep, salt air and forced myself to calm down as much as I could. I had been so wound up since Susan disappeared, I hadn't let myself stop. And all of this morning I had been plain scared. But now I was here. I was alive. And I had people to find and a thousand more questions to ask Susan.

But first, it seemed the most logical thing I should do was get inside, out of the wind and the cold. I took one more long look at the ocean and then went over to the pack. I grabbed it by the shoulder straps and half carried it, half dragged it in the direction of the rope barrier.

As I came near the rope, a door opened in the bulkhead and two men came out. One was wearing a decorative uniform indicating he was one of the ship's crew. The other wore a thick turtleneck sweater. They were talking about something to do with the operation of the main card room.

"Excuse me," I said as loud as I could, so they would hear me over the wind and the low rumble of the ship's engines.

Neither man looked up.

"Hey! Excuse me!" I shouted again. All I wanted was a little information as to where I might check in. or whatever a person was supposed to do when they came through one of those mirrors.

The two men walked right past me, the officer missing me by less than an inch. Neither gave the slightest notice that I was standing there.

I watched them as they ducked under the rope and went through large double doors into what looked like an open, carpeted area. Through the wooden, paned windows, I could see them move across the room and start down some stairs.

Something wasn't right. I forced myself to stop and really look around. I had seen pictures of cruise ships. They were sleek and modern. This one looked elegant, but in the fashion of an old home instead of a new ship. Those windows had thick drapes framing them. The stairs inside had wrought-iron and wood-sculptured railings. The lifeboats were huge and made of wood. No modern cruise line would do that. Of course, I don't know why I expected this would be a modern cruise line. Alex had been gone since 1909, so it would seem logical that it might be an old ship. But with one glance, anyone could tell this ship didn't show the wear of time. This was a new ship with an old design.

I glanced up at the flags flying in the stiff breeze near the front of four smoke stacks. Four smoke stacks? Something about that struck a bell in my head, but I couldn't quite grasp the memory. One of the flags looked British. The other had a white star.

I dropped the pack and went over to the nearest covered life boat. There, stenciled on the canvas cover were the words RMS TITANIC.

I was going to be sick. I could feel the huge lunch Constance had fed me twisting in my stomach as I tried to deny the possibility of my being on the *Titanic*. I rubbed my hands across the words and then quickly went down the deck and checked the next boat. It was the same. This was either one huge joke or I was on the *Titanic*.

What the hell was going on?

I looked slowly and carefully around. The strange coats and dresses the passengers wore were straight from the early part of the century. So were the ornate wood carvings along the windows, the wooden deck chairs, the thick drapes. And the officers' strange uniforms. Everything fit the *Titanic*.

Except me.

Susan had said the mirrors took people to places where they were held. Why would the mirror stick me on a ship that was going to sink? Punishment? Maybe a test? Or an intermediate stopover?

It made no sense. I must have been sent to a different place, and time, than Susan. What had I done wrong?

Holy Christ, I was on the *Titanic*. I leaned against the rail and looked around at the ship. For me, the *Titanic* had been an obsession. I think I had read everything ever written and watched every movie ever made about the ship and that night it sank. The shock waves of this ship's sinking had been felt throughout the world. I had never stopped being totally fascinated by its myth.

So what was I doing on it? Was this just a trick my mind was playing on me? That was a possibility. Was I really still sitting there in the lodge?

I'd better be finding some answers damn soon.

I went back over and grabbed the pack and somehow swung it up so that both straps were on one shoulder. Then I shifted its weight around so that it rested on my lower back. I could make it a ways, but I doubted if I could walk the entire length of the ship. I figured my best bet would be to go into one of the main dining rooms and find someone who would be willing to answer a few questions. Seemed logical enough.

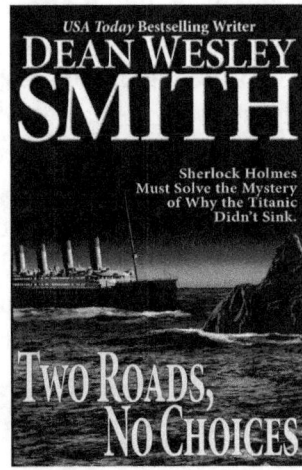

I followed the same route the two men had taken earlier and went through the huge double doors.

Inside, I found myself looking down at the top of the grand staircase.

The only clear word for the grand staircase was *impressive*. It could easily have been the center of an English castle, or a southern mansion. But instead it had been built on a ship.

Reverently, as if I were a small child entering an ancient cathedral, I moved over and ran my hand along the polished oak and wrought-iron rail. It felt warm and smooth to my touch, almost alive. Below me, the wall above the stair's first landing was covered with a wooden sculpture of two figures holding a crown over a clock. I could remember reading an article about that very sculpture and the story behind why it was there. But right at the moment, I couldn't remember the piece's name.

The clock read 7:30. What day? Another damn important question. The ship sank at 2:20 in the morning on April 15. I just hoped this wasn't the evening of the fourteenth.

I spent the next few minutes easing my way down the huge staircase to the next deck, holding on to the rail to keep the pack from tipping me over. At least a dozen passengers passed me and not a one even noticed I was there, or even glanced at me because of my strange clothes or overloaded backpack. By the time I got to the bottom, I was pretty well spooked by that fact alone. And absolutely convinced I couldn't go another step with the pack.

I moved off to a corner where I figured I would be out of the way and eased the pack down to the thick carpet. I was amazed I hadn't hurt myself trying to carry the stupid thing. I leaned it against the oak-paneled wall. The pack was going to stay there until I found some answers.

I studied the large, high-ceilinged foyer. I was in the first-class section of the ship. On both sides of the foyer were wide double doors that led outside to what must have been the "A" deck. To my left was a five-person-wide, carpeted and windowed hallway. Most of the people seemed to be heading or coming from that hallway, so I dropped in behind a young couple and followed them.

A door to the right opened into what looked to be the first-class reading room. I stayed behind the couple and went through the oak and glass double doors at the end of the hall into a large, open room.

I was stunned by the beauty of the room. Twenty-five to thirty people sat at tables or lounged on couches, talking, laughing, or sipping drinks. Thick, patterned carpet, oak chairs and tables, polished wood columns, and thickly draped, paned windows. I stood there in the doorway with my mouth open, staring. It wasn't until two men rose and started at me that I moved out of the way.

"Excuse me," I said. Both men were dressed in striped three-piece suits. The one on the left was taller, maybe my height. The other man was short and heavyset, with a thick, black moustache. Both totally ignored me.

"Pardon me," I said a little louder as they came near me. "Could you please tell me—"

They walked right on by, the tall man brushing past me and holding the door open for the other man. Neither one acknowledged my presence. It was as if I were invisible. Hell, for all I knew, maybe I was. Or more likely, I was just making all this up in my own head.

I took one more look around the huge lounge and then turned and followed the two men. If they were going to ignore me, the least they could do was lead me around for a while.

They headed down the right side of the grand staircase. I did a quick check to make sure my pack was still where I left it, then followed.

The next deck down looked very much the same as the one above, except without the hall on the right. Instead, across the open foyer at the bottom of the stairs were two wooden doors that led down halls to rooms. The two men went around to the right and continued down. I stayed about five steps behind them, listening as they talked of the medical problems of their wives. It seemed that both their wives were always complaining about some sickness or another.

The next deck was like the one above it and the two men didn't hesitate for a moment before going around and down the right-hand stairway. So far, in two flights of stairs, I had passed a good fifty passengers and a dozen stewards. Not one of them had looked as if they might belong to a time other than 1912. And not one of them noticed me, or even so much as glanced in my direction.

The next deck was considerably different than the ones above it. The bottom of the grand staircase opened out onto a large, ornately furnished room with at least thirty oak tables surrounded by upholstered armchairs. Less than a dozen passengers sat at the tables, most of them over near the windows on the port side.

The short man made a comment about how their wives must already be seated and both men headed for a double door on the far side of the room. I remembered from my reading about the *Titanic* that the first-class saloon, or dining room, was through those doors.

It was the largest single room on the ship, capable of holding over two hundred diners at one time, all eating elegant meals, served at the highest of society's standards. I almost beat the two men to the door in my eagerness to see that famous room.

And it was everything I had ever imagined it to be. Handcrafted oak chairs, linen-covered tables, ornate wood columns, deep oak paneling on the walls. The air was full of rich food odors and the sounds of people talking, silverware clinking against plates, and ice swirling in fine crystal.

I moved out of the doorway and stood and watched as an army of waiters catered to every whim of over a hundred people at once. The two men I had followed went to a table near the center of the room and sat down with two women. After a few minutes, another party of six people entered from the port-side entrance and were seated at another table near the center. The maitre d' who had seated them headed in my direction, looking stern. Finally, someone had noticed me.

But I was wrong. He walked right past me and through the doors into the waiting area and the grand staircase. That scared me. The way I was dressed, in a ski parka and jeans, I should have at least gotten a dirty look from a man used to everyone wearing fine clothes to dinner. I quickly followed him back into the waiting area to his small desk.

"Excuse me," I said, standing in front of his desk. "Could you tell me what day this is?"

He didn't even look up.

"Hey, I asked you—" I reached forward to touch his arm. My hand went right through him and touched the desktop ledger instead.

I thought I'd been shot.

Not only did my hand pass through him, but he must have been wired with electricity. I got a jolt that sent me staggering back across the room and into a table. I suppose I should have sat down right at that moment, caught my breath, and thought everything through. But I didn't. It didn't even cross my mind.

Instead, I turned and ran.

It took me no more than ten seconds to cross that large room and get up those stairs. At the next deck, winded, sweating, scared, and my heart again threatening to jump out of my chest, I slowed down to a walk. But I didn't stop until I got back to my pack two more decks up.

There I slumped down on the carpet with my back against the oak paneling.

I wasn't moving until I got my head clear and I felt rested. For the next half hour I sat and watched the steady stream of ghosts climbing up and down the grand staircase.

Or was I the ghost? Either way, I had gotten myself into big trouble this time. It hadn't just been the shock from the maitre d' that had sent me running. As I reached for him, I had caught a glimpse of the date on his ledger.

April 14, 1912.

Unless the mirror pulled me off real soon, in a few hours I was going for one very cold swim.

To be continued...

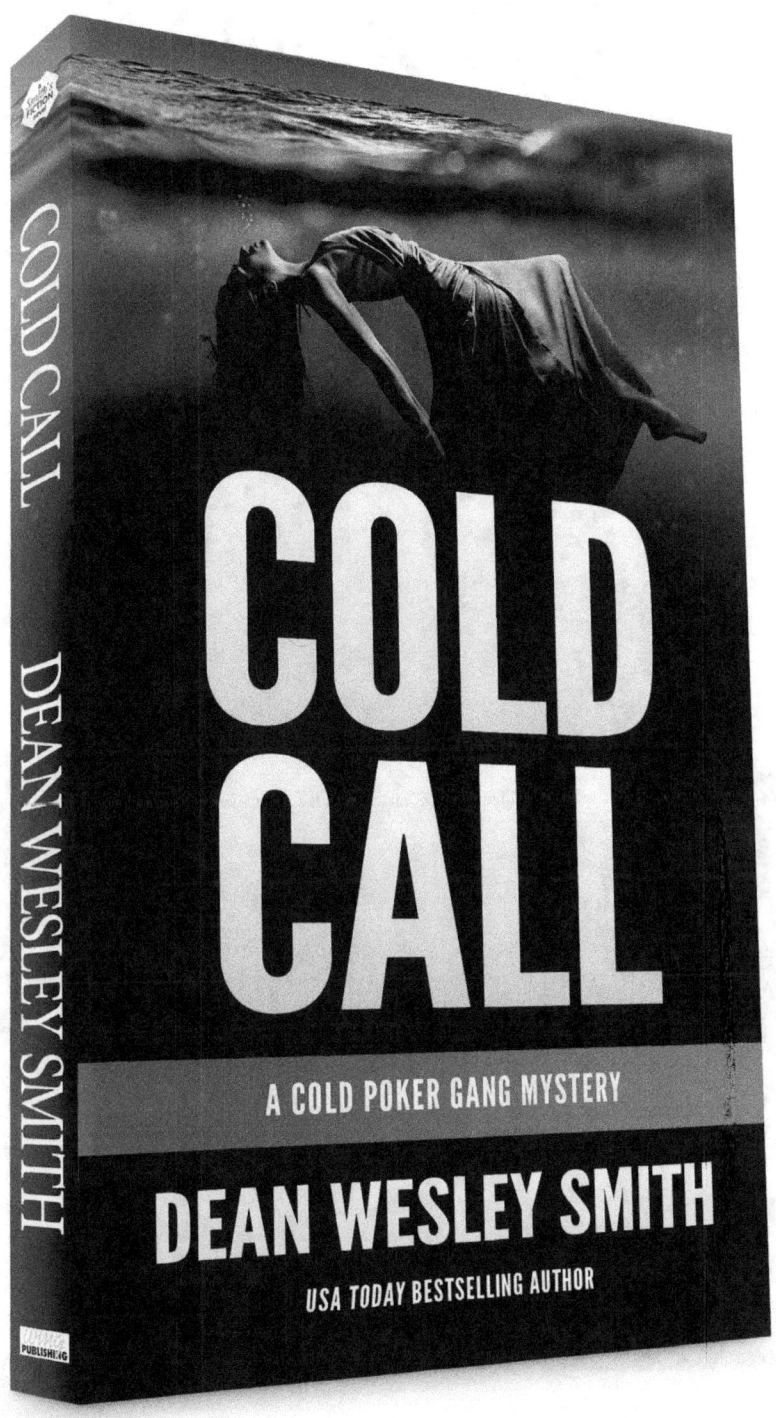

USA Today Bestselling Writer
DEAN WESLEY
SMITH
BEST EATEN
ON A SLOW TUESDAY

Mark Estes flaunted his money, abused his power, cheated on his wife, and most of all loved to eat.

Warned that a dozen sugar cookies would kill him, he ate them anyway.

So how would Mark Estes deal with the ultimate diet challenge?

A story that answers the simple question: Do diets come from hell?

BEST EATEN ON A SLOW TUESDAY

MARK ESTES STARED at the sugar cookies in Heaven's Bakery window. The grains of white sugar seemed to catch the light of the sunny, spring day at just the perfect angle, making the cookies almost twinkle in happiness.

Cookies could be happy, couldn't they? They made him happy just looking at them.

The sidewalk in front of the bakery smelled like fresh bread, drawing unsuspecting passersby like him to the evil trap of sugar cookies and a promise of how they would melt in his mouth with their joyous sweetness.

He knew he would be transported to his own heaven if he could just bite into one or two of them.

No, maybe in the end a half dozen or so.

No. No. He would need a dozen.

A baker's dozen.

Thirteen of the little bastards would give their lives to his taste sensations and they would die happy doing so. He wouldn't even share them with his mistress, Candy. He would eat them before he got to his secret penthouse apartment for their normal Tuesday lunch romp on the Posture Perfect Mattress. Neither Candy nor his annoying diet-master of a wife, Beth, would ever know.

Secret cookies were a lot better than flaunted cookies.

Both Candy and his wife stayed with him because of his money. And his power. He had no doubt they were both afraid to leave him. And they should be. He hadn't gotten to where he was at in the world without a few broken bones and bodies in his wake.

So if he wanted to spend some money on sugar cookies, screw Candy and his wife and his stupid doctors.

Cookies were worth it.

Good food of all types was worth it.

He just loved to eat, almost more than anything else in the world.

He hitched up his silk pants and checked his suspenders to make sure neither had come loose under his silk jacket. He seemed to be gaining a little weight, so he was going to need to get new suits this week. As long as he kept his suits fitting his 400 plus pounds, no one would notice he was still gaining weight.

He glanced around, feeling slightly guilty, but not enough to turn away from the wonderful bakery smell. Then, as he started for the front door, his phone rang.

He pulled it from his pocket and glanced at it. Only three or four people on the planet had his private number. Shit, it was Brenda, his secretary. She had strict orders to never call him on Tuesday and Friday lunch breaks unless it was an extreme emergency.

He answered, "Yeah. Better be good."

"Sir," she said. "I have really bad news."

"Go ahead."

She took a deep breath. "A dozen sugar cookies will kill you this afternoon at 3:15 p.m. exactly."

"What?" he asked.

"Don't have the sugar cookies, sir," Brenda said. "Just go have sex with Candy and come back to the office. I beg of you."

He actually sputtered.

Mark Estes, one of the most powerful men in all the city prided himself in not being caught unaware or surprised.

And he never sputtered.

Never.

He clicked off the phone without another word, then made sure the tracking on the GPS was switched off, then he turned the entire phone off and stuck it in his pocket.

Then slowly, he stood in front of the window with the plate of sugar cookies and studied the neighborhood around him, looking for anyone suspicious, or anyone watching him.

Third Street was wide, with cars parked on both sides and two lanes of traffic headed east in the middle. As was normal for midday, the traffic was heavy, mostly cabs, and the sidewalks had a fair share of people focused on getting somewhere and ignoring everyone else.

A number of office buildings towered over the street, with storefronts, delis, and restaurants lining the sidewalk on both sides. His office was on the top floor of a building two blocks from here. His company owned the entire thirty-story building. His secret penthouse apartment was still another three blocks away.

On bad weather days he had his limo driver take him the five blocks, but today because the weather was nice, not too hot, not too nasty, he had decided to walk.

His business was the importing of condiments for half the country. He was rich beyond his imagination and had seldom cared what anyone thought or said about him. Or his massive weight.

At five-eight, four hundred pounds made him look round and more powerful than he already was.

All he cared about was getting more power, bossing around other people, eating great food, and having sex like a whale of a bunny.

So how did Brenda know he was going to buy cookies and what was all this scare crap about the cookies killing him at a specific time?

He liked Brenda, he trusted Brenda. Maybe it hadn't been Brenda who had made that call.

In this modern world, anything was possible, especially with the Democrats in charge. He had sure donated his fair share to some questionable Republican candidates. Maybe that was what this was all about.

He shook his head. No one scared the condiment king off his cookies.

He took out his phone, clicked it on, and called his office.

Brenda answered.

"How did you know about the cookies?" he asked.

"What cookies?" she asked.

"Did you just call me a minute ago?"

"No, sir," she said. "I respect your orders to not be disturbed."

"Thank you," he said. "I will be back by 3 p.m."

"Very good, sir," Brenda said.

He clicked off his phone again.

So he had been right, it hadn't been Brenda who called him. He would get his security people on it when he got back to the office. He had some top-notch people working in his tech department. They would be able to tell who had hacked his phone.

He glanced at the plate of sugar cookies once again. The little bastards called

to him even more. He needed to buy two dozen, keep a dozen for snacking in his office.

He again started for the door of the bakery and his cell phone rang again.

But it couldn't ring. It had been turned off.

He pulled it out of his pocket.

It wasn't turned on, but it was ringing anyway.

Now that was some fancy hacking skills.

"What do you want?" he said to the phone without putting it up against the side of his head.

Text instantly appeared on the screen. "Don't eat the cookies. They will kill you at 3:15 p.m."

"Fuck you," he said to the phone, walked three steps and tossed the phone as hard as he could at the pavement in the gutter. Then he stepped on it with his polished new shoes, smashing the damaged phone into bits.

A couple walking past gave him a wide berth and muttered something about anger management courses loud enough for him to hear.

He stood on the edge of the street between a parked Ford Taurus and an old pickup truck with most of its paint missing. He was panting and he could feel his heart racing.

When he got back to his office, he would have a team of tech experts track through that private phone account. No one hacked him like that. No one.

Suddenly, at that moment his stomach rumbled.

He glanced back at the bakery and the cookies in the window. The fresh bread smell seemed to have gotten stronger.

He needed cookies, then sex.

In that order.

And that's what he got.

In that order.

He made it back to his office with the second dozen cookies in a white bag just five minutes after three. Candy had been her own wonderful and energetic sex partner, letting him mostly just lay there while she did all the moving around his bulk.

He liked that.

And he had flat loved the cookies. They had delivered on their promise of life-altering sweetness and melt-in-your-mouth death.

He had savored them, eating the last one while on the elevator to his apartment.

Although, after the cookies, the sex, and the walk back to his office, he was feeling a little washed out. Luckily his afternoon was pretty light on appointments.

Brenda nodded to him as she handed him his messages as he walked past and into his office.

He had dropped into his chair before he realized someone was sitting across the desk from him.

It took him a moment to recognize the large bulk of his best friend Benny Nieto. The two of them had come up through school together, both built businesses, and remained fast friends through it all right up until the day Benny had died two years before of complications from diabetes. He had only been fifty-two.

Benny's death had caused Mark to cut back eating for a short time, start walking more, and get a physical. It was during that physical that Mark had learned that he was also diabetic.

Beth, on hearing that news, had become a tyrant around food, as she said, trying to keep him alive.

After a few months of food hell, he had just decided to play along, but not bother.

"You're not here," Mark said to Benny.

"Yeah, I know, I'm dead." Benny said, biting into what looked like a huge peanut butter cookie.

"So I know you're dead and you know your dead, how come I can see you?"

Benny shrugged letting the flesh on his massive shoulders jiggle like he was experiencing an earthquake. "I'm just waiting for 3:15 so we can get the hell out of here and go have dinner."

"Ghosts eat?" Mark asked, ignoring that time thing again.

"The restaurants on the other side are to die for," Benny said, then realized the bad pun and laughed, again sending waves of flesh bouncing around his body.

Mark had no doubt that Benny had gained some weight since dying. A lot of weight, actually. Hundreds of pounds, maybe.

"So it was you that tried to get me to not eat the cookies?" Mark asked.

"Sure was," Benny said. "If you hadn't eaten those cookies, you could have gone on banging good old Candy for another six years before the heart attack finally got you."

"But how?" Mark asked.

"The overload from the cookies to your system is going to shut you down in about three minutes. You die almost instantly."

Mark felt a bolt of terror surge through his body. "Any way out of this?"

"Nope, not after you ate those cookies," Benny said. "Suicide by sugar. But I bet they were good, huh?"

Mark ignored him.

"Sorry old friend," Benny said. "We both picked this path through the world and out the door. We knew what we were doing. And you enjoyed those cookies, as much as all the other meals and desserts you have eaten. We both traded off years of life for food. Sometimes I think it was worth it."

"Only sometimes?" Mark asked, glancing at his watch.

"The food is great on the other side," Benny said. "You'll see in just a minute."

"But it has its problems?" Mark asked.

"Oh, sure," Benny said, finishing off the peanut butter cookie. "No hookers and no money, so no woman on the other side is interested in anyone our size except the really creepy ones with some really sick stuff going on."

"Okay," Mark said. "So what's the downside?"

Benny held up his hand. "Say good-bye to that living body."

Mark suddenly felt a sharp pain run through his entire body and the next thing he knew he went face-first into the expensive cherry wood of his desk.

Then, he stood up and moved to one side, feeling almost exactly the same.

His human body was solidly encased in his big chair, his face slack-jawed and his eyes open, staring into nothingness.

Mark looked down at his ghost body. He was still wearing his silk jacket and pants, held up by suspenders.

Benny slowly pushed himself out of his chair and stuck out his hand. "Welcome to the other side."

Mark shook it. "Thanks for coming to meet me."

They both stood there staring at Mark's body for a moment. He didn't feel at all sad about dying. He felt nothing, actually.

Benny handed him a peanut butter cookie and Mark took a bite. The taste was heavenly, even better than the sugar cookies that had killed him.

"Does all food on this side taste this good?" he asked.

"Sure does," Benny said. "You up for getting some lunch?"

"I am," Mark said.

Benny shifted his massive bulk toward the office door. "Follow me."

Two Thunder Mountain Short Stories
Available at your favorite booksellers.

"We can't just jump to where we want to go?"

Benny laughed. "Nope, we walk everywhere. And it doesn't help us lose a pound either."

"Is that the downside you mentioned?" Mark asked as they made their way past Brenda, who was staring at her computer screen and didn't notice the two large ghosts.

"Nope," Benny said. "The downside is that we use no energy, burn no fat or calories when we move around or just exist each day. But we take in calories when we eat."

Mark shook his head. He wasn't understanding at all what Benny was getting at.

Benny finally reached the staircase and walked through the door.

"No elevator?" Mark asked.

"Can't," Benny said. "Elevators, cars, trains, nothing works for us. We walk. And let me tell you, it took me all morning to climb these stairs to meet you."

"Thanks," Mark said.

"Don't mention it," Benny said. "That's what friends are for."

"So besides the walking and not burning any calories, what's the downside you mentioned?"

"For a time I thought of it as an upside," Benny said. "On this side of death, we don't pee or crap."

"That's a downside?" Mark asked. At 400 pounds, both of those bodily functions had become chores.

Benny made the ten steps down to the first landing and stopped, panting and red in the face.

Mark felt the same way. Going down stairs was almost as hard as climbing them.

"Think it through," Benny said. "All in, nothing out."

"You mean we are just going to get fatter?"

"Unless you don't eat anything at all," Benny said. "But I don't think I could spend eternity doing that unless I was forced to."

Mark sat down on the steps and stared at his best friend. What Benny was saying was finally dawning on him.

"We're going to eat and get so fat we can't move around anymore because we

don't burn calories and can't pee or shit," Mark said. "Is that what you are saying?"

"Yup, spot on the nose," Benny said.

"And then we spend eternity as giant blobs of flesh only thinking about food, but having no way to get any. Right?"

"That's how I read it as well," Benny said.

Mark just put his head down and covered his face with his hands. He could feel he was hungry. He wanted another peanut butter cookie. More sugar cookies. Steaks, seafood, you name it, he wanted it.

He craved it.

And the feeling was very real.

He pushed the feeling away as best he could and tried to think. He had died and now, to keep his ability to even begin to move around as much as he did now, he had to stop eating.

Period.

Or he could eat until he could never move around again and then never eat after that, craving food for all eternity.

This was hell. He had no doubt.

He always sort of knew this was where he might head considering many of the things he had done to get ahead. But he had always kind of hoped there wouldn't be either a heaven or a hell.

He had been wrong about that.

"Any out you can see on this?" Mark asked.

Benny shook his head. "There are massive piles of human flesh all over the place, existing where they fell and couldn't get up."

"Oh, Jesus," Mark said.

"He doesn't live in these parts," Benny said. "But what's even worse are the poor souls who got sent here on the other side of things."

Now Mark was confused.

Benny clearly saw that.

"You'll understand when we get to the street. The people who are in this place who were focused in life only on staying thin with the same passion that we ate don't get fat here. They burn calories when they move around, but take no calories in no matter how much they eat."

Benny just shuddered. Exactly the opposite of what was going to happen to them.

"Piles of living human bones litter the street as well," Benny said, shaking his head in disgust. "Nothing but skin covering bones. They just stay where they fell when some muscle finally got eaten away from starvation."

"So we are all destined in this hell to go one direction or the other?" Mark asked.

"Got it in one," Benny said.

Mark felt his stomach rumbling. "So you say the food is great here?"

Benny nodded, smiling. "Memorable."

"Memorable enough for the memories of the food to last for eternity?" Mark asked.

Benny made a motion to indicate his huge mass of flesh. "I'm betting on it."

Mark could either go on a strict diet and never eat and retain the right to move around or he could eat and then remember each meal off into eternity.

Short-term gain, long-term loss.

That's how he had gambled with his life when alive. He could see no reason to change now.

This was hell. Of that there was no doubt.

But at least the food was good.

And the cookies heavenly.

~

DEAN WESLEY SMITH

SHE LOVED HER DRINK
MAYBE MORE THAN LIFE

MAKE MYSELF
JUST ONE MORE

A Mary Jo Assassin Story

Mary Jo kills people for money. After a thousand years, she knows patience and skill and how to cover her tracks.

Mary Jo loves her job. She makes a lot of money as a hired assassin.

She also loves vodka and orange juice. Passionately, but not in a dangerous way. After a job well done, she rewards herself with the drink.

Mary Jo might be the coldest killer in all of fiction. Or at least the only really cold killer who loves vodka and orange juice.

MAKE MYSELF JUST ONE MORE
A Mary Jo Assassin Story

MARY JO STOOD, staring at the bottle of Smirnoff Vodka in her hand. She had a pitcher of orange juice beside her on the counter, ice was a touch away in the fridge, and a highball glass sat waiting.

She was fairly certain she could have just one more.

She thought she had done everything right.

The granite surface was spotless, the white cabinets wiped down completely, the floor scrubbed.

Not a spot of anything could have survived in this kitchen. She had even opened every door and make sure nothing had dripped down onto a hinge or in a crack. She had sanitized every tiny inch with bleach.

She had put nothing down any sink, but instead used a plastic bucket for the cleaning water. Then outside in the fenced backyard she had washed the bucket out completely in the gravel at the back end of the path to the yard.

Then she had put the bucket in the ground in a new flowerbed she had planted last week. She had punched some holes in the bottom of the bucket, put a new plant in the bucket, and filled the bucket up with dirt completely.

The bucket was covered completely. It was gone.

Then she had turned on the sprinklers that watered the lawn, including the area of the path where she had poured the cleaning water.

She was very good at this sort of thing.

Mary Jo never expected anything to lead back to her and this house, but it made no sense to take any chance when just a little bit of work would solve any problem.

Then she had gone into the guest room, put her blouse, bra, underwear, jeans, shoes and socks in a black trash bag along with all the cloths she had used for the cleaning and set the bag near the back door.

Then she had gone to her own bedroom upstairs in the four-bedroom, two-bath suburban home, taken a shower, making sure she was clean.

Extra sure. Especially her short brown hair.

She had liked this house in the year since she and Bob had gotten married. It kind of fit a part of her that she didn't often get to enjoy. And she could play the perfect housewife role to a science. She was only five-five, had short brown hair that made her look more like a pixie than anything else, and a body style with narrow hips and a small chest that didn't show any of her strength.

She was a member of an ancient order of assassins. She had lived for thousands of years, as everyone in her order tended to do. And she had never grown tired of her job. Ever. In fact, the job had gotten more challenging as technology improved.

She liked that and the money it supplied her to live a lavish lifestyle.

After her shower, she had dressed in a similar white blouse that she had had on earlier, same style of jeans, underwear, everything, including a second pair of sneakers.

With a pair of white gloves on, she took the black bag and put it into the back of her Jeep Cherokee along with a couple bags of normal week's garbage. She had set this routine up a year ago. This was all normal for her, including the white gloves. She had then driven the thirty minutes to the landfill just outside of town.

There she had made sure every bag was tossed over the edge of the dumping area into an area full of other black bags that a bulldozer was moving around and covering in layers of dirt.

She had paid the attendant in cash and he hadn't even noticed her other than to nod hi as he did every week. His attention was focused on the two pickup trucks behind her full of junk.

Now she was back at her house looking at the bottle of vodka and orange juice and wondering if she dared have one more drink.

After all, it had been the first Screwdriver with just a little too much vodka in it that had started all this mess and then cleaning.

Actually, it hadn't been, but it was fun to think that it had.

She loved her drinks, but was very careful in the thick of a job to not drink too much.

As she stood there, staring at the fixings for a drink she felt she wanted but wasn't sure she needed, her cell phone went off.

It was her husband's ring.

She answered it. "Hi, honey."

"Afraid I'm going to be late for dinner," he said. "Got a body."

"Oh, no," she said, making herself take a deep breath. Her husband was the lead homicide detective for the entire city. This call was normal. Over their year of marriage it had happened a good thirty times.

She had been responsible for a few of those bodies, just as she was for the one that had just been found. But he never knew that and never would.

"I'm sorry to hear that," she said. "How about I wait for you and we go out to Murphy's Diner when you are done."

"Might get late," he said.

"I'll snack until you call."

"That would be nice," he said. He told her that he loved her and then hung up.

He was a good man. She had enjoyed the year plus they had been together. The sex had been good, the laugher real. After centuries of living and killing, she had learned to appreciate those times even more.

She glanced at her watch. It was a quarter after four. The timing was spot on the money.

She glanced at the bottle of vodka one more time, then set it aside, put the pitcher of orange juice back in the fridge and the clean glass back in the cabinet.

Maybe after her dinner.

She then took her purse and went out to her Jeep. The third row of seats was always down in her car so she could carry gardening and groceries easily.

She lifted the seat and there was the bag with a rifle in it. Her disguise bag was there as well.

She slipped on her gloves for a moment and did a quick inventory to make sure everything was with the rifle and the disguise bag and she hadn't forgotten anything, then lowered the seats back into place.

Fifteen minutes later she had parked her Jeep in the mall parking lot out of any camera sight. She then, when no one was around, transferred her rifle to the small Ford four-door sedan backseat and locked the car. The car was brown, with plates mostly covered in mud.

The Ford sedan had been stolen by a man she had never met and left for her. She had paid the man ten grand for the car in a drop bag. He hadn't asked questions.

Then, carrying her disguise bag, she went into the mall and into the public restroom as herself. She came out almost forty minutes later, after dozens of other women had come and gone, as a long-haired blonde with a much larger nose and a tan jacket and red tennis shoes.

She walked to her car not drawing any attention to herself, climbed into the brown sedan and fifteen minutes later had it parked on the top of a pine-tree covered hill just to the right of town.

She had turned the car around so she could go straight down the hill she had just come up and be lost in the streets below in thirty seconds, long before anyone below even knew what hit them.

She left the car running and left the disguise bag in the car. She then took her rifle and made sure it was loaded.

It was a deer rifle, a classic bolt-action Roberts with a scope. Actually the rifle was a collector's item that she remembered back sixty years really liking. The thief who had given her the rifle had assured her it was accurate and had been tested.

She tested it on him and he had been right, actually. The thief was still one of her husband's unsolved cases.

She moved to the small stone wall that kept tourists on this hill from tumbling over the edge of a fairly steep cliff down into an old quarry below. This small turn-around often held teens out parking for some first love experiences in a parent's car.

She was so old now, she could barely remember her first sexual experiences. They had not been pleasant, she remembered that much.

The quarry two hundred feet below was abandoned and mostly a playground for neighborhood kids after school and in the summer.

The body of good old Sam lay below her, right where she had dumped it three hours before.

Sam had been handsome in his own right for forty. He lived with his wife Becky three doors down the street from her and stayed home days to work on a novel. Mary Jo had asked him to help her with a wiring issue in her porch light that she had created. She told him it had sparked and she was afraid of a fire starting.

He had fixed it, they had laughed, she had offered him a Screwdriver in payment for his hard work, and then she had stabbed him in the back, perfectly through his heart with a long ice pick as he moved to get ice.

His blood mostly had pooled on the floor around him, but she had still cleaned everything to make sure.

She had sipped her first drink of the day as he lay dead on her kitchen floor.

She loved Screwdrivers. Best drink ever as far as she was concerned.

Killing never did anything for her, one way or the other, and poor old Sam was just bait for her husband who was the real target.

She checked the area in the small clearing around her to make sure no one was nearby that she would also need to

kill, then eased up over the edge of the stone wall and looked down.

Sam's body was now covered.

Her husband stood with two other detectives in a tight group near the body, talking.

Good, she would take care of all three at the same time. First her husband, who was her target, the one she was getting paid to kill. She had slept with her target for fourteen months. She thought of it like a cat playing with a mouse.

She studied the scene quickly one more time. By taking out the other two detectives, it would slow down any investigation.

"Goodbye, dear," she said softly. "This is what you get for pissing off the wrong people who have far too much money."

The rifle was loud, but had almost no kick. The echo of her first shot bounced around through the trees and over the surrounding farmlands.

Her husband went to the ground instantly.

She knew the entry wound would be small in his chest, but most of his back would be blown away from the high-velocity rifle as the hollow point bullet expanded on impact and blew him apart.

She quickly took out her husband's best friend and partner with a second shot before anyone even thought to move for cover.

She killed the third detective as he turned to run.

She picked up the three shells, made sure she had left nothing else where she had fired, then put the gun back in the case on the back seat of the car and headed down the road.

She turned away from the police and then worked her way slowly back toward the mall.

She parked the Ford sedan next to her Jeep again. Then transferred the disguise bag and everything into her car and put the rifle back under the back seats.

She climbed into her Jeep and turned on a high-tech scanner she had in her purse that told her if any camera was watching at all.

Nothing, as she had known for this area of the large mall parking lot.

She quickly pulled off her disguise and tossed them into the bag, zipping it up and putting it on the floor behind her driver's seat.

Then she took off the thin, transparent gloves she had been wearing that were embedded with fake fingerprints and stuck those in the pocket of her jeans.

Back at home, Mary Jo put back on the fake fingerprint gloves and pulled out two more black garbage bags full of weekly trash from the kitchen, including a bunch of stuff she had tossed out of the fridge after wiping prints and putting the fake prints on the stuff.

Then she got the rifle from the car and broke it down and put parts in three bags, wearing her fake fingerprint gloves as she did.

Then she took parts of her costume and spread them through the garbage as well. And she made sure that there was nothing in the bags that would lead to her in this home in any fashion.

Then she headed back to the landfill, made some mention to the man taking her money that it was her second trip because she was cleaning house. He didn't care.

And she tossed the three bags over the edge and into the stinking mess of the landfill.

A moment later the large grader covered all three with a layer of dirt.

Mary Jo then went home to wait to play the part of the grieving widow.

Sam's wife would be grieving as well tonight.

She was watching television two hours later when two uniformed cops came to her door.

One was a woman cop who seemed to be almost in tears.

They told Mary Jo the news and she broke down as the two cops expected her to do.

They asked Mary Jo if there was anything they could do and Mary Jo told them she had a sister who would come over and stay with her. She didn't, but the two cops bought it.

Then the woman cop hugged her harder and longer than was necessary and gave Mary Jo her card for anything she needed.

Mary Jo wondered if her good old husband had been getting a little of that on the side. He didn't seem to be the type. But that had sure been a strange hug.

Mary Jo was about to go fix herself that long-overdue second Screwdriver after the two officers left when her alarm bells went off.

Instead, she went to her bedroom and stripped down and climbed in the shower, all the while pretending to be distraught.

Finding nothing attached to her body, she came out and used a scanner she kept hidden in the back of her dresser drawer to check for bugs.

The woman officer had planted one all right, under the back collar of her blouse.

Audio only.

There were no other bugs in the house.

No young rookie cop would do that, especially so quickly after the entire department was tossed into panic mode. Besides, there was no reason to suspect her.

That girl worked for someone outside the department. More than likely the same idiot who had paid Mary Jo to kill her husband and would pay a second half as soon as she reported in to him.

And now he would pay a far higher sum. You didn't try to double cross Mary Jo. Not ever. The idiots who had hired her had no idea the order of assassins even existed.

Keeping up the act of a distraught wife for the bug, she put her blouse back on with her jeans and tennis shoes. Then she put on thin, clear gloves and took from what looked like a perfume bottle a small drop of fluid on a pad. She carefully wrapped the pad in a tiny bag and stuck it in her pocket. It was an odorless, untraceable poison that would kill anyone who touched it within five minutes.

Then she called the young officer. "I want to see my husband."

"I don't think that is such a good idea," the young woman cop said.

Mary Jo nodded. Both of them were right on script.

"I'm coming to the station anyway," Mary Jo said.

Fifteen minutes later, she pulled up out front after pretending to cry most of the way to the station so that anyone listening to the bug wouldn't be shocked.

The young cop met Mary Jo at the big double door. Concrete steps led up into the front desk of the station.

"I don't think this is a good idea," the young cop said. "He was shot and they need to do an autopsy."

Mary Jo had the poison pad in her hand and her hands were covered in the thin gloves. "You may be right. I don't know what I am thinking."

She gave the young cop a hug, rubbing the pad along her neck before backing away.

"I'm sure sorry," Mary Jo said.

"It's understandable," the young cop said.

Suddenly the young cop looked pale and swallowed hard.

Mary Jo took her under her arm and turned to take her up the three steps and into the station. The drug was very fast acting and this woman would be dead in five minutes tops.

As she did, Mary Jo took off the glove and tossed it into a garbage can near the front door full of Burger King cups and food bags. The poison wouldn't last in the air like that for another thirty minutes and the gloves would dissolve in two hours.

"Help!" Mary Jo shouted to the officers inside as she opened the door. "She just collapsed into my arms on the front steps."

Two cops ran to grab the young officer, then a third nodded to Mary Jo and offered his sincere condolences.

Mary Jo broke into sobs, as scheduled for her part of this passion play, and they let her sit in a back office and calm down before having an officer drive her home.

Then Mary Jo killed the bug on her blouse and made sure the rest of her house was clean of all recording and electronic devices.

It was.

She dug out a burner phone from a fake bottom of her purse and dialed a number.

"Yeah," a voice on the other end said.

"Target is dead. The remainder of my fee has tripled because of your attempt at a double cross. If the money is not in the agreed-upon account by this time tomorrow afternoon, you know the consequences."

"You can't threaten me," the voice said.

"I know where you live, where your children sleep, where your wife loves to eat sushi," Mary Jo said. "I am patient, invisible, and you hired me because I get the job done. The job you hired me to do is done. The price is now four times my fee. Please do not fail me."

Then she hung up, put the phone in a baggy and smashed it into tiny pieces.

Then she put some bleach and a few drops of a special solution into the baggy, sealed it, and tossed it into the trashcan outside. The entire thing would be a puddle of goo in the bottom of the can in an hour.

She then took a deep breath.

Finally, it was time.

She took out the pitcher of orange juice, a highball glass, and the vodka. She filled the glass with ice, added a good solid shot of vodka, then filled the rest of the glass with orange juice.

Then she put everything away before sipping the wonderful drink.

Perfect.

Just perfect.

Maybe, just maybe, a little later, she might just have one more.

After all, a grieving widow could be forgiven a drink or two.

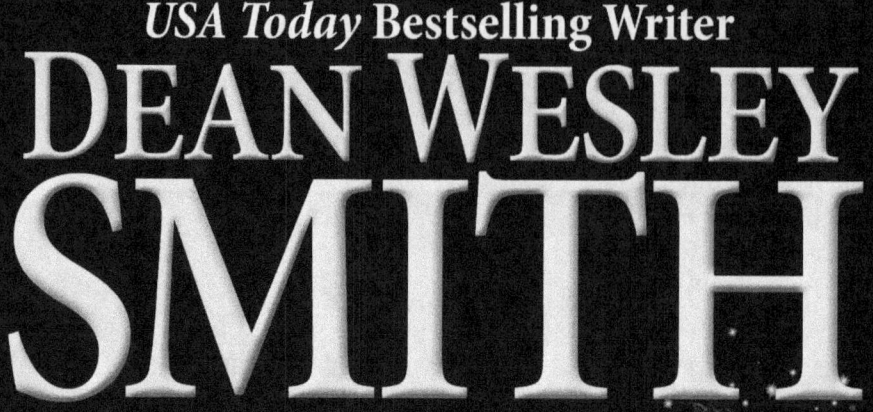

USA *Today* Bestselling Writer

DEAN WESLEY SMITH

When Cleaning
the Garage,
Information Happens

WHY DELAY?
JUST RUB

Weird things happen on Bryant Street. Even when cleaning a double-car garage.

Late spring, very little sports on television, weather threatening to rain so no golf for Jack. Time to clean out the garage.

Also time to find the old lamp in a pile of garbage. Of course, Jack rubs the lamp to try to clean it.

And on Bryant Street, that means the entire chore of cleaning out a garage snaps into strangeness.

A twisted tale of a man, a wife, and a dirty garage as only can be told on Bryant Street.

WHY DELAY? JUST RUB
A Bryant Street Story

JACK HAD FINALLY, after a year of promising and far, far too much gentle nagging and reminders from Connie, his wife, agreed to clean out the garage.

The June day was dark and overcast, threatening rain. Not a day he wanted to be on the golf course anyway. And June sports sucked on television.

Really sucked unless you loved baseball.

So cleaning out the ten years of accumulation and dirt and dust in the large two-car garage finally hit the top of the priority list just because there was nothing better to do.

Nothing.

Absolutely nothing.

And it would buy him some husband points in the great game of marriage.

Jack thought of himself as an average man in the scheme of things. He didn't much mind that. He had started his own accounting firm that now had two offices and five accountants working for him. So he was a successful average guy.

He kept himself in moderate shape for forty years old, with only a small gut and a slight balding spot on the top of his head. He mostly kept himself in shape by walking on nice days from his office to lunch and then on the golf course on weekends. Plus Connie was a sensible cook so he didn't overeat.

Jack actually never did much of anything in excess. Excess was just not his style.

He didn't smoke and drank very little and then only socially and on weekends.

And had been married to Connie since college and had never even thought of straying with another woman.

He had the best woman in the world as a partner, why would he?

They had two kids in college now, both staying in their respective schools during the summer to work part-time jobs instead of coming home. Both had promised they would be home for the 4th of July, which had always been a big deal for Jack. He liked the patriotism and the fireworks, although he wouldn't allow his kids to ever have any fireworks. Just too dangerous.

Connie, his wife, still looked stunning at forty. She was thin, with short brown hair and a wide smile that people liked. She was the funny one of the two of them. The one with the sense of humor; the one that people liked to talk to.

She could charm a group of people in minutes.

She went to the gym every day during the week and owned her own clothing store in the local mall that was doing very well. She had been talking with him about opening a second store and he could see no reason why not.

To Jack, Connie was the dream girl of his life, always had been, always would be. He had no idea why she stayed with him, but she seemed to like their quiet life and routine.

Sometimes he worried about that. Worried about her being with him. But only sometimes.

Again, he never did anything to excess, including worry.

When he had finally agreed to clean out the garage, Connie was excited. She had bought extra trashcans for the job and a lot of extra big black trash bags as well. Plus a number of spray cleaners and a box of rags usually used when painting.

Jack was fairly certain that the garage wasn't that dirty or had that much trash in it. But he never complained when Connie over-prepared for anything. It was one of the many things he loved about her.

He opened both doors to the wide driveway. They had a large four bedroom, three-bath home in a nice subdivision not too far from downtown. He drove a blue SUV and Connie drove a green minivan. Both cars were sitting in their normal parking spaces on the driveway. Neither of their cars had seen the inside of the garage in five years.

Maybe it was past time to do this chore.

The neighborhood looked quiet for a summer Saturday afternoon and the sky had darkened. The air had a calm, muggy feel about it and if he had been a betting man, which he was not, he would bet the predicted rain wasn't far off.

Connie had put on a long white apron over her slacks and white blouse and had slipped on an old pair of running shoes. She pointed to an area beside the garage. "We'll stack the trash there and I'll have it picked up next week."

"A good idea," he said, looking at the piles of stuff for the first time in years with actual natural light on the subject. Where had they gotten all this crap?

More than likely much of it was from the kids.

"We put the stuff still good enough to donate here when we get a spot big enough," Connie said, pointing to a spot near one garage door on her car's side. "I'll have someone come to pick it up next week as well."

"Perfect," he said.

She handed him a pair of work gloves and then pulled on a pair herself.

"This is going to be fun," she said.

That he was convinced would not happen, but it would get done. And that would free up a bunch of time on nice weekends for golf.

They both started on the same pile, mostly pulling items that they both knew were trash and bagging it. And he had been right, most of the trash was from the kids. Leftover parts of their lives that now he and Connie were just bagging and tossing to the curb.

Interesting how that happened with children.

And then, when he and Connie were gone, the kids would come in and toss their lives to the curb. The cycle of things.

After a while, he and Connie had a spot cleared enough to start stacking some items that looked like they could be good enough to donate to a local charity. If it ended up being enough, it would be a nice tax deduction.

If nothing else, he was always the accountant.

Two old kids' bikes started that pile. Then a box of dishes from their first apartment. Opening that box had made them both laugh. The dishes had the worst flower patterns on them that he had ever seen. He had hated those dishes and thought they had vanished a decade ago.

Well, now they would be gone.

Then he found a half-molded old cardboard box and opened it.

Inside was a stack of old pans, some strange metal figures, and an old metal lamp. It looked like it was copper, dented and tarnished, and had the shape of a lamp from India.

"Where did this come from?" he asked, pulling out the lamp and holding it up. It seemed empty and there wasn't a wick in the spout end.

Connie shook her head and came over closer to look. "Not a clue," she said. "More than likely something one of the kids found and brought home for some reason. Maybe as a prop in one of their plays."

He nodded. That made sense. Both his kids had done plays all the way through high school. Costumes and props were always coming home with them.

He was about to toss the beat-up old lamp on the charity pile when some printing on one side caught his eye.

He rubbed off the dirt to see what it said and damned if smoke didn't come from the top of the old lamp, everything froze around him, and a tall guy with some sort of turban on his head appeared out of the smoke. The guy wore big, baggy pants and had on no shirt.

And wow, did he have some muscles.

"Wow, nifty prop," Jack said. "Connie, take a look at this."

When he glanced over, she was frozen in place, a hand reaching for something in the pile, her face smudged with some dirt.

Jack glanced back at the tall guy with his arms crossed like a Mr. Clean commercial standing in his garage.

The guy looked real.

How bad of a cliché was this?

"Connie, nice joke!" Jack said, turning back to her.

She hadn't moved. No one, even in good shape, could hold the position she was in for more than a few seconds.

"Who are you?" Jack asked the big, impossible man standing in his Saturday cleanup project.

The man pointed at the lamp still in Jack's hand.

Jack glanced down at the lamp. On the side the words read, "Rub me once for the Genie to appear, rub me twice to get a wish."

Jack quickly set the lamp down and went over to Connie. She was still in the same position.

He moved her arm in closer to her body. He could move her just fine, so he went into the kitchen, got a chair and brought it out and worked her around until she was sitting down.

The guy was still standing in the garage, his arms crossed over his bare chest.

Jack went back inside and tried to call the police, but all the lines were dead. Nothing at all was working.

Everything was frozen.

He went back out to the guy and just stared at the hunk of man.

He flat didn't believe the guy was a genie, but he was going to play along with the gag until someone started laughing.

"Can you talk to me, answer questions?"

The man did not move. He just kept staring straight ahead like there was something real important on the garage wall.

Connie kept sitting on the chair. She hadn't moved at all.

Jack went out to look up and down the street and that was when he saw a few raindrops just hanging in the air.

Time had really stopped around this guy.

Oh, shit!

How was this possible?

Genies in lamps didn't exist in American suburbia. They existed in old fairytales and kids' books.

Jack reached up and touched one drop of water with a finger. It didn't move.

And nothing was supporting it.

"Shit! Shit! Shit!"

Jack seldom swore, even on the golf course, but he figured this time if any was appropriate.

He moved back around the big man with the cloth on his head and carefully picked up the lamp.

Nothing had changed.

And there was no writing on the other side or on the bottom of the old thing.

He set the lamp down carefully on the concrete garage floor and went back into the house to get a glass of water and try to think.

Of course, the water wouldn't come out of the tap and he couldn't get the fridge open.

He was going to have to rub that stupid lamp to get this to end.

But none of this could be happening. Magic wasn't real. This had to be an illusion of some sort.

But if it was real, what should he wish for? He had seen enough bad movies and bad cartoons to know that wishes from genies never turned out as well as hoped.

He sat down at the kitchen table and looked around the house. What would he wish for? He had a beautiful wife he loved, a great home, enough money.

And if he said he wished for nothing, that might be how he ended up.

So he had to be careful. If this was real, which it seemed to be, he needed to ask for something innocent.

But what?

What did he really want?

He could ask for a better golf game, but he wouldn't feel right about that because the fun of golf was in the chase, not just suddenly, magically being better.

He flat couldn't think of anything.

He stood and went back out into the large garage.

Connie was still sitting in the position he had left her. She looked even more beautiful than before, even with the smudge on her cheek.

He had no idea why she stayed with him.

And then he realized that question had been bothering him for a long, long time. They had a comfortable relationship, based on family and familiarity and habit.

Was he nothing more than a habit to her?

He finally had the chance to know.

He picked up the lamp, then carefully thought through his question and rubbed the lamp solidly.

The genie's large dark eyes focused on Jack.

"Your wish?"

"I do not understand why Connie, my wife, has stayed with me for all these years. I would like to know if she has ever had an affair with another man or woman while we have been married?"

"No," the genie said. "She has not."

Then the genie laughed, a sound that Jack was certain might break a few windows if it got louder.

As smoke started to come from the lamp and swirl around the genie, the big man shook his head. "You two really need to get a life. And that's coming from a guy who lives in an old lamp."

"Why?" Jack asked.

The genie shook his head. "She asked the exact same thing about you."

"She did?"

The genie laughed again. "She doesn't understand why you have stayed with her all these years either. Try talking more, would you?"

Then he was gone.

And so was the memory of the genie being there.

Outside the garage door, the rain was just starting to fall.

"What am I doing sitting down?" Connie asked, looking around.

Jack had no idea. He just tossed the lamp into the charity pile and went to her.

"I ever tell you how beautiful you are?" he said as she sat there, looking very stunned.

She laughed and stood. "Nice try, mister. How did I get sitting there on one of our good kitchen chairs?"

"Don't ask me why you are lounging around," he said. "I've been sorting through junk."

He kissed her and turned back to the shrinking pile. It would be nice to get his car back in here again. He had to admit that.

And besides, on a rainy summer afternoon, what better thing was there to do than spend the day with the love of his life, no matter what he was doing.

A big, booming voice inside Jack's head said, *Now that's better.*

Then Jack thought he heard a laugh, but it was actually only thunder in the distance.

~

USA Today Bestselling Author

DEAN WESLEY
SMITH

IDANHA HOTEL
A Thunder Mountain Story

May: 1902. Megan Taber bakes in the fancy new Idanha Hotel in downtown Boise. Her rolls and pastries and pies bring in patrons from all around the area.

Widowed from her husband five years before, her entire life focuses on her baking. And she loves it. She considers baking her art.

Joe Vaughn, a scholar, eats breakfast every day at the Idanha Hotel dining room because of Megan Taber's baking.

A story of two people, tossed together by events and great food.

IDANHA HOTEL
A Thunder Mountain Story

ONE

May 28th, 1902
Boise, Idaho

MEGAN TABER'S PASSION was baking. At five-ten and barely only one hundred and ten pounds, she didn't look like a typical baker, but around Boise in 1902, she was known as the best there was.

And she loved what she did. She worked at the Idanha Hotel, the fancy new place that had only been open for just under two years. It boasted the best restaurant in the entire state and she was proud to be a part of that. And from what she understood from reviews she saw in major papers, her pastries and cakes and pies had made the hotel restaurant one of the best places to eat in the entire west.

She often worked from sunset to sunrise to have enough breads and cakes and desserts ready for a day in the hotel, but she didn't mind at all. Baking was her life.

She was widowed from Janson Taber two months after they had married and moved to Boise. He fell from a ladder and hit his head and never woke up. That had been seven years earlier, when she was only eighteen. She now seldom thought of him.

She had made her own way, without a husband, and she was proud of that fact.

She had spent the last seven years learning how to bake, how to be the best. She read all the magazines she could get from the East and talked with every elderly woman she could about their recipes that they would talk about. She studied baking like scientists studied the stars or nature. She was passionate about it.

To her, baking was not only a science, but an art. Of course, she never said that to anyone.

She had worked at a few other restaurants around town, getting a reputation as the best baker of any kind of bread, pie, or cake there was in all the West.

When the Idanha Hotel was scheduled to open their doors, Chef Pickner had offered her the job, with great pay and a furnished apartment in the hotel. She had jumped at the chance.

She had had job offers since for hotels and restaurants in San Francisco, but had always told Pickner she would stay with him as long as he wanted her.

So her baking drew in many, many a diner at the Idanha restaurant with her bread that seemed to melt with buttery deliciousness in a person's mouth and her pies and cakes that were heavenly in taste.

And if it was up to her, the Idanha was where she would remain the rest of her life.

If not for a series of lucky circumstances, the rest of her life might not have been that long.

Two Thunder Mountain Novels
Available at your favorite booksellers.

On the early morning of May 28th, the air still had a bite to it, but to Megan it felt wonderful after being so long around the hot ovens in the kitchen. After her nights baking were done, she almost always went out onto the rough boards of the sidewalk on the west side of the hotel to just get some fresh air and sometimes enjoy the sunrise over the mountains to the East. It helped her clear her mind so she could take a long bath and then sleep with her drapes drawn through much of the day.

This morning, she felt a little more light-headed than usual. She hoped she wasn't coming down with something.

She leaned against the large stone of the hotel wall and made herself take deep breaths.

As she stood there, a gentleman by the name of Joe Vaughn came from the direction of the stables. She knew he usually took his breakfast in the Idanha Restaurant and numbers of times had sent her notes complimenting one of her breads or desserts.

She pushed away from the wall, standing as a lady would stand when meeting a gentleman on a sidewalk in public.

She had actually never met Mr. Vaughn, but she knew him by reputation as a gentleman, single, her age of twenty-five, and a scholar who lived out in Warm Springs. She had never heard what he was studying.

As he neared and she could see him up close, he was more handsome than she had heard. He had a square chin, dark eyes, and a smile that seemed to light up his eyes. If she hadn't already been a little faint, more than likely his looks would have caused it.

He had on a three-piece suit and a small black hat. He tipped his hat to her and smiled. "Miss Taber, the honor is all mine."

She knew she still had on her apron and more than likely had flour in her brown hair that she kept pulled back and tied. But that was who she was and there was no point in putting on airs.

She bowed slightly and somehow managed to get her mouth to speak, even while staring at his handsome face and bright smile. "Mr. Vaughn, thank you for the compliments. I treasure them."

"And I treasure the wonderful art you put into your pastries and breads," he said. "I have traveled a great deal and have never seen the likes of what you do. You are why I ride into town every day for breakfast."

"I am very honored," she said again, bowing slightly. She could not believe that he also thought of what she did as an art. How wonderful was that, someone who understood and appreciated.

She was going to say something along those lines when the world around her started to spin and she felt a pain in her chest.

"I seem to feel a little…" she said, her voice trailing off.

And then everything went black as Mr. Vaughn looked shocked and stepped toward her as she fell.

TWO

May 28th, 1902
Boise, Idaho

MEGAN AWOKE IN the hospital. The smell of piss and blood almost gagged her. And her chest hurt as if she had been stepped on by a horse. A woman with dark black hair and a stained uniform that had been white at one point was sitting beside Megan, clearly monitoring her.

Megan tried to sit up, but the nurse instantly held her from doing so. "You can't be moving. Your heart will not stand for it."

"What happened?" Megan asked, her voice dry.

The nurse gave her a sip of water that felt wonderful.

"About an hour ago you fainted on the sidewalk in front of me," a male voice said from the other side of her bed.

She turned to see Mr. Vaughn standing with his hat in his hand, looking worried.

"Did you bring me here?"

"I did, along with two of the staff at the Idanha," he said. "They needed to return to work, so I told them I would report in on your condition."

"Thank you," Megan said, now feeling even more embarrassed that such a gentleman had to have been bothered by her.

"I hope you don't mind," Mr. Vaughn said, "but at the institute I reside out in Warm Springs, there is a major heart doctor from the East who happens to be visiting. I have asked him to come take a look at you."

"I don't think that will be necessary," Megan said.

"It is," the nurse said. "Your heart is not sounding good so we want you to have the best care."

Megan looked at the stern, but clearly concerned nurse, then back at Mr. Vaughn. "Thank you."

He smiled that wonderful smile of his. "My desire to help is purely selfish, of course. A breakfast without your wonderful bread would not be the same."

She smiled back, but didn't have the energy to even say thank you again.

A moment later she was asleep and back in the blackness.

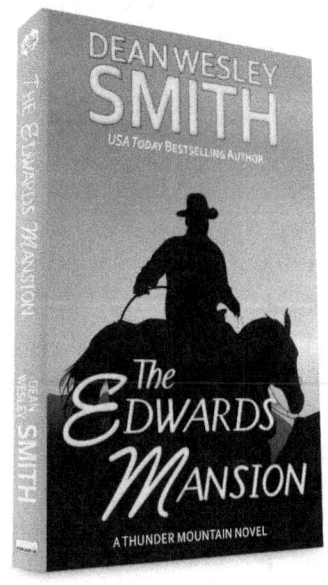

THREE

May 28th, 1902
Boise, Idaho

MEGAN AWOKE THE next time in the back of a buckboard as it eased over a large bump in a road.

Two men sat beside her. One was Mr. Vaughn, the other was a stranger she did not recognize.

"She seems to be waking up," Vaughn said.

Then he looked at Megan. "We are doing our best to save your life. Please, please hold on."

With that, the other man put a cloth gently over her nose and mouth and once again she fell into the blackness.

FOUR

September 2nd
Boise, Idaho

MEGAN ONCE AGAIN awoke, but this time to the sounds of strange beeping. Her chest hurt worse than she could ever imagine, but at least she was still alive.

She opened her eyes to stare at a very white ceiling that seemed to have a lot of tiny holes punched in it.

She blinked twice and the ceiling with the tiny holes did not go away.

She was as thirsty as she could ever remember being. And there was a sour taste of almonds in her mouth.

Something was stuck up her nose, but she didn't have the energy to see what it was.

Beside her the beeping continued like nothing she had ever heard before.

She tried to turn to see what the infernal beeping was, but the pain made her moan.

She heard movement and a man suddenly appeared in her line of sight. He was dressed in a strange shirt with no collar, like an undershirt of some sort with writing on it, and he had a smile on his face.

It was Mr. Vaughn.

"Welcome back," he said. "We thought we lost you there for a time."

A woman in a white uniform appeared to Megan's left and gave her an ice chip that she could suck on.

The ice chip felt like heaven. Wow.

"I'll tell the doctor she is awake," the nurse said.

Mr. Vaughn nodded. Then he turned to Megan, his expression suddenly very serious. "You are going to see things in the next day or so that you do not understand at all. I promise you that I will answer all your questions, so do not ask the doctors or nurses. Just ask me when we are alone."

She looked at him.

"This is important," he said. "Promise me? Just know that you are in a hospital and had an operation that saved your life. This is a very advanced hospital. I will explain everything. I promise."

She nodded.

At that moment a man came in. "Glad you are awake, Miss Taber. You gave us all a scare there for awhile."

Megan said nothing as the man in the white coat shined a tiny light in her eyes, then listened to her heart for a moment through an instrument, then nodded.

"We are going to need you to be up and walking this afternoon," he said. "It will be painful, but it will be important. The nurse and others will be here to help you."

She nodded. Then through her cracked and dry throat she said, "Thank you."

He smiled. "Don't thank me, thank Mr. Vaughn and the others at the Historical Institute. They somehow managed to keep you alive long enough for me to fix your heart. But that said, you are more than welcome."

He smiled and then turned and left.

"Just rest," Mr. Vaughn said.

Megan nodded and closed her eyes and went back into the darkness.

FIVE

September 6th
Boise, Idaho

FOR MEGAN, THE next two days after her operation were a series of naps, extreme pain when trying to walk, and no dignity at all as a nurse had to help her in the bathroom. A hovering and smiling Mr. Vaughn were her only bright moments that she remembered at all.

Mr. Vaughn had been right. Most of what she saw made no sense to her. Of course, she had not been in a hospital before. When her husband died, a doctor had come to see him, make him comfortable in their own home, and then when her husband had died, she had him taken to the mortuary.

But for the first two days after the operation, she had been too tired and in too much pain to even ask about all the fancy machines and tubes in her arms and up her nose and so on. And after that, they just became normal, part of how she was living.

And she was going to have a pretty good scar on her chest from what she could tell from the ugly incision that had to have the dressing changed regularly.

Every morning Mr. Vaughn was there, waiting for her to wake up and he spent the entire day with her, helping her walk the halls, talking with her and promising he would not make her laugh, even though he did at times, which hurt like all get out.

She was growing very fond of him and he clearly felt the same way toward her. She had no idea why she deserved such intense attention from such a gentleman, but she was very thankful for it.

After four days, she was doing a lot better and making some good laps around the hospital corridors every day with Mr. Vaughn. And she was doing her best to figure out just what some of the strange and bland foods were that they were forcing her to eat.

Mr. Vaughn called it "pretend food" and she tended to agree.

By the afternoon of the fourth day, they had moved her to what they called a regular room. It was on the same floor, just down the hall a ways.

And it had a window looking out onto some branches of some trees. She could see the birds flitting back and forth in the trees and hear them in the morning, which made her feel even better.

Every morning, the wonderful smile of Mr. Vaughn cheered her up as well. And he had been insisting that she call him Joe. She had agreed only if he called her Megan.

Now every time he called her Megan, she smiled even more.

When she got moved into the private room, two others came to see her. She recognized them both as regulars in the Idanha Hotel, often coming for breakfast or dinner.

Vaughn introduced them as Bonnie and Duster Kendal, the founders of the Historical Institute.

Duster wore a long oilcloth coat, a dark matching hat, and boots. But Bonnie had on something Megan had not seen before until the hospital. She had on a white blouse, a nice necklace, and jeans with some sort of canvas shoe. She looked very comfortable and at ease in the outfit, even though out in public, as others had looked who had come into the hospital.

She liked both Bonnie and Duster at once and at one point Duster asked her if Joe had been answering her questions about all the strange things.

"She hasn't had any yet," Joe said, smiling.

"Better that way," Bonnie said, laughing. "More than enough time to ask questions once you get out of this place."

"My thoughts exactly," Megan said.

SIX

September 10th
Boise, Idaho

EIGHT DAYS AFTER her operation, Megan was feeling a lot stronger, but still needing a lot of help. She could sit up for a while and walk pretty good distances. It would still be some time before she could get back into the kitchen, but thanks to Joe, she would be able to eventually.

"They are going to release you from the hospital today," Joe said, smiling as he came into her room. "Bonnie and Duster are going to come and help get you back to the Institute where you can live and recover."

"Couldn't I go to my apartment?" she asked.

Joe looked very worried. "Remember what I told you about seeing very strange things and that I would answer your questions?"

She nodded. "Some of the people coming in and out of this hospital have been very strange."

He smiled at that. "Now that I agree with."

"But there is more, is there not?" she asked, looking into the worried eyes of the man she had come to really like over the last few days. More than she ever thought possible after the death of her husband.

"There is a great deal more," Joe said, nodding. "And we will try to explain some of it on the way to the Institute. And all of it over the coming days. We will be bluntly honest with you, I promise."

"You can't tell me now?"

"I think seeing will be believing in this case," Joe said. "And just remember, we had to bring you here to save your life."

She nodded, not liking the sound of that at all. But at this point, she was just along for the ride, as they say.

Late that afternoon, after she had combed out her long hair and left it flowing down her back and had dressed in new underwear and jeans like Bonnie wore and a light blouse also like Bonnie wore, Duster and Bonnie walked in, all smiles.

"You are sprung," Duster said. "All bills are coming to the Institute and everything is settled."

"You don't need to do that," Megan said. "I am sure I can work off my bill in time."

Bonnie laughed and patted her hand. "We have more money than anyone has a right to have. It is the least the Institute can do for you and Joe."

"Thank you," Megan said. "I do not know how to repay you."

"Oh, trust me, some of that bread you baked at the hotel was repayment enough," Duster said.

"Here, here," Joe said.

And Bonnie nodded. "Tough to keep a girl's figure with your fine treats."

Megan just smiled. When her baking was appreciated, the day was a good one. That's how she had always felt.

"I'll pull up the car at the front door," Duster said.

"Okay," Joe said as Megan settled into the wheelchair and Bonnie and Duster headed out into the hallway ahead of them. "Here come all the really strange things I warned you about. You ready?"

"Not at all sure what I should be ready for," she said.

"Fantastic sights and things that you could never imagine before," he said.

At that they went down the hallway, saying goodbye to the wonderful nurses and a few of the doctors, out through some double doors she had not been through before, and then into a very modern elevator, very, very different from the Otis in the Idanha Hotel.

And a moment later, after a very smooth ride that almost did not feel like movement at all, the doors slid open and Joe pushed her out and turned toward a double door made almost entirely of clear glass.

"So Duster has a new-fangled automobile?" Megan asked as they headed for the door.

Joe laughed. "It's new all right. But new to this year."

She glanced back and up at Joe as they neared the front door and she could see strange cars passing by on a road on the other side of a wide lawn.

"What do you mean this year?" she asked.

"You had a major heart attack in 1902 that would have killed you within a day," Joe said. "To save your life, I brought you forward in time one hundred and eighteen years to the year 2020."

At that, the wide glass doors in front of them opened like magic and he pushed her into the warm, afternoon air.

Around her, she couldn't make much sense of anything.

Smooth, white surfaces led off in all directions and a large acre of fancy, modern autos were parked side-by-side. Trees and plants and flowers were planted in orderly fashions all around her, making the area very beautiful.

On a paved street beyond the large acre, cars went by at unthinkable speeds without seeming to collide in any fashion. That looked frightening to her.

There was a low rumbling noise and then off to her right, she looked up to see a massive mechanical object that looked a little like a soaring hawk floating through the air.

"What was that?" she asked, pointing at the huge thing that seemed to stay in the air without reason.

"That's an airliner that carries hundreds of people from city to city and all around the world through the air," Joe said, kneeling down beside her chair so he could see her face.

"Oh, my," she said.

Her mind was spinning and she took a deep breath of the fresh afternoon air. The spinning slowed.

"We are about five miles outside the old downtown area of Boise," Joe said. "Boise now has almost half-a-million people living here. And this hospital you have been in is one of the best in the West."

She glanced back up at the building overhead that towered far taller than any building she had ever seen in her life. It seemed to be made of metal and glass and gleamed in the afternoon sunlight.

Then she looked at Joe who was looking very worried.

"You brought me into the future to save my life?" she asked.

"I did," he said, nodding. "I am from this time and was only living in the past to do research on a project I am working on. I fell for you the moment I saw you and just couldn't stand the thought of you dying from something that in my time could be fixed."

She took a deep breath of the warm air as Bonnie and Duster pulled up in front of them in a massive automobile, far larger than most wagons of her time. It seemed to run almost silently.

As Joe had warned her, she was not going to understand.

She didn't. Not in the slightest.

He had promised he would explain it all to her. She assumed that included how she got from 1902 to this year in the future. She trusted him.

She looked directly at him again. What she did understand was the look in Joe's eyes of worry and caring and attention. That didn't seem to change with time.

He was in love with her as much as she had fallen in love with him.

That was really all that mattered.

"I am sure I will learn all about this time," she said after taking another deep breath. "As long as I can bake."

"Your art has not changed hardly at all over the years," Joe said. "You would be a master in any time."

She smiled. He sure knew how to say the exact right thing.

She had fallen in love with him. And it was far, far more than just the fact that he had saved her life.

She turned slightly to him. "Can you lean in closer?" she asked, as Duster and Bonnie started to climb out of the huge automobile. "I want to stand."

He did, a worried look on his face as he helped her out of the wheelchair.

She turned in his arms and looked him directly in the eye. "I just wanted to say thank you one more time before I start asking a million questions."

And with that, she kissed him, something a woman of her time should never do.

And after a second, he kissed her back.

And that kiss felt even better than she might have ever imagined.

In any year.

Now Available
from all your favorite booksellers in trade paper and electronic editions.

USA Today bestselling author Dean Wesley Smith brings back the Slots of Saturn in this short novel from the popular series featuring the superhero Poker Boy.

Poker Boy and his team destroyed the Slots of Saturn. They know they did. At least, they think they did.

But when people begin disappearing—again—poker boy must face what might just prove his greatest foe.

THEY'RE BACK
A Poker Boy Short Novel

CHAPTER ONE
Not Possible, but Fact

"THE SLOTS OF SATURN are back," Stan, the God of Poker said to me as he slid into the booth beside Patty.

I laughed and pointed out the window. "Pig just flew by. Pink, a ribbon on its tail. Really flapping hard."

Patty giggled and shook her head.

Stan said nothing, didn't even laugh at my stupid joke.

"Wait, just saw another."

Again he didn't laugh or even shake his head in disgust, which he often did when I got really silly.

Both Patty and I just stared at him, waiting for his punch line. He had just said that the Slots of Saturn were back. That had to be a joke with a really stupid punch line, because those monsters were not a laughing matter.

But no punch line was coming, at least none that I could tell. Trying to get a read on the God of Poker was just about impossible. He had the best poker face on the planet and with his tan slacks, button-down brown cardigan sweater and short brown hair, he could make himself invisible in a crowd without any powers at all.

"Sorry, Poker Boy, Patty," Stan said. "I can't believe it either."

"Serious?" I asked. "No flying pigs with pink ribbons?"

"Serious," he said.

Patty and I had been having a quiet lunch in my invisible office, floating high over the Las Vegas strip. I should have known a wonderful day like today would have a crisis in the middle of it.

Just not this crisis.

Any crisis would be fine except this one.

Patty and I were both dressed in casual jeans and light shirts to spend the day together, since she had a day off from her job at the MGM Grand Hotel front desk. I still had on my black leather coat and fedora-like hat that was my uniform as a superhero. I just didn't feel comfortable going many places without them.

We had plans to tour the Mob Museum that both of us had wanted to see for a year, but hadn't found the time. Then we hoped to have a nice dinner and then go back to her apartment, watch a movie, and see what happened next.

I had been looking forward to that "next" part of the plan all morning.

And lunch in my office had seemed like a great way to start a relaxing and fun day together.

My invisible office floated a thousand feet over the Las Vegas Strip and consisted of four walls of windows and a diner booth smack in the middle of the room. The red vinyl booth had soft seats and could hold eight around the table with room enough for another two to pull up chairs on the end. It was patterned after Madge's imitation 1960's diner my team had met in for years down near Fremont Street in downtown Las Vegas.

An invisible door led from Madge's Diner to this office so that Madge, the waitress (who was also a superhero in the food service part of the gods) could wait on us in here. It was also the entrance for those without teleportation powers.

My office actually served as more of a clubhouse for the members of my team more than anything else. Sitting up here at night on a chair with your feet up on the railing looking out over the city and The Strip was always amazing and relaxing.

After hard days, a lot of the team members did just that.

There was also another invisible door that led to Patty's apartment where we stayed while in town. When we completed our new home we were building in the Oregon Coast Mountains, I would put in a direct door to this office from there as well.

Since Patty didn't teleport, that would allow her to get back to Vegas anytime she wanted from our new home in Oregon.

Patty Ledgerwood, aka Front Desk Girl, was my sidekick and partner and the woman of my heart. We met the first time The Slots of Saturn ghost slots had attacked the city. And we had been a pair ever since.

Now it seemed the ghost slots were back.

Not possible, just not possible.

I just wasn't going to let myself believe it yet.

Madge came through the door from the diner with my cheeseburger and Patty's salad and a big basket of fries. She had already brought us both a large vanilla milkshake to share and had Stan's favorite strawberry shake on her tray as well.

She slid lunches in front of us and gave Stan his shake. Then she slid the fries over to an open spot at the end of the table and turned to leave without saying a word.

The fries only meant one thing. Laverne, Lady Luck herself, was on the way and had ordered ahead.

So the ghost slots really were back, even though that was completely impossible.

A moment later Screamer, the other original member of our team, and Ben, the oldest and yet newest member of our team appeared and slid into the other side of the booth facing me and Patty.

Screamer had taken part when we rescued over a hundred people from near death in the Slots of Saturn the first time. But wow, that was a long time ago.

Ten years ago, to be exact.

Screamer had the ability, among other things, to get into someone's head and read their thoughts and transfer those thoughts to others. He was a superhero working on the law enforcement side of the gods.

Ben was a god himself, just as Stan was. Ben had been the God of Lamplighters for centuries, but as they didn't need lamplighters as a profession anymore, he had faded. He had spent a lot of time over centuries reading and he remembered every detail. I got him moved over to work with the Gods of Books and Libraries to get him healthy again, and he had became a critical part of our team. He knew history and he knew all the politics and history of the gods. I couldn't believe how much he had helped us so far.

"So what Stan said is true?" I asked, looking at Screamer.

"We got ten people missing so far," Screamer said, nodding, "and my sources with the police think it might be a few more."

"But how?" Patty asked, her voice sounding as stunned as I felt. "We all three stood there outside that warehouse and watched those three slot machines be hauled off to be crushed and destroyed."

I glanced at Stan, who only shrugged. "We don't know, but we've seen security images of the Slots of Saturn appearing and taking someone and vanishing. Just as they did the first time. Exactly, actually. Same spots in the casinos. The locations they appear, that we know about, we now have blocked off."

"So they really are back?" I asked, the fear crushing any idea I had of taking a bite out of my cheeseburger, no matter how good it smelled.

"It seems that way," Stan said. "And we checked and they are not returning to the old Standard Machines warehouse."

"So we don't have any idea where they are stored this time?" I asked. That was how we had managed to deal with them the first time. We found their home.

"No clue at all," Lady Luck said, appearing and pulling a chair up to the table. She didn't grab a fry, but instead just sat there, staring at me.

And when Lady Luck just stares at you, that is not a good sign.

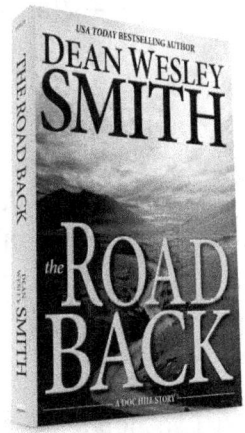

CHAPTER TWO
Searching for a Clue in the Past

GHOST SLOTS HAD been a myth or urban legend in Las Vegas since slot machines started to become popular. The myth was that a person could pour their entire soul into the machine and thus vanish into the machine.

In other words, slot machines took the souls of people.

I had walked by enough people glassy-eyed in front of slot machines over the decades to think there was some gems of truth in those legends.

And then ten years ago I discovered ghost slots were very, very real when the Slots of Saturn started to attack.

The Slots of Saturn were a three-seat set of very old, very tall slot machines with incredibly-beautiful images of the rings of Saturn all over the machines. You actually had to pull the handle and coins rattled out into the metal tray when you won. They were old machines, retired in the late 1980s and stored in a giant warehouse called a "graveyard."

That's where we had found them through an incredible series of lucky events and teamwork. That day the team had managed to save over a hundred people from the ghost slots.

And we thought we had killed the slots.

Seems we hadn't.

The next two hours we all sat there in the booth, trying to figure out what to do next.

A couple times Lady Luck popped out to check on something, and Stan at one point agreed to talk with the Bookkeeper to see if he could get projections on the machines, assuming no one was controlling them.

Stan said the Bookkeeper was working on it when he came back and would call if he got some results.

The Bookkeeper was a god in the numbers area who never left his house or his computers. He could work a computer and research through the internet faster than anyone in existence. And he had an amazing talent of projecting events that would happen in the future using just numbers.

If someone had learned how to control those deadly slot monsters, then nothing the Bookkeeper could do to project their appearance would help. But if, like the first time, they were just runaway machines hungry for power from those who fed them, aka humans, then they could be predicted.

And the Bookkeeper could do it.

When they took a human, they jumped back to their original location. Then on some hidden schedule that only the Bookkeeper and all his computers could project, the machines would jump again to a location, wait for another victim to sit down and pull the old handle, then with the victim trapped inside the machine, jump back to their original location.

The one limitation ghost slots had was that they could only go back to a place they had occupied in a casino at some point in the past. The problem was that in those days, slots were moved around from casino to casino all the time.

Records of slot movements were hard to find, hard to follow, or had been destroyed by now. There just didn't seem to be much of a reason to save where old slot machines had been thirty or forty or fifty years before and in old buildings now torn down.

Finally, after two hours, Patty and I and Ben were the only three left in the booth. Madge had long since taken away my partially eaten cheeseburger and brought Patty and me another vanilla milkshake.

Lady Luck had jumped off to talk with the gods of law enforcement to see what the real total of missing people might be.

And from exactly where.

Screamer had gone with Stan to talk with the only remaining slot machine tech who had been part of that rescue ten years before. The slot repairman who had triggered the first attack of the Slots of Saturn was now dead.

The three of us were in a wait-and-think mode.

Ben looked like anyone's standard image of the perfect grandfather. Short and square, dressed in a suit without a tie, with short gray hair and a receding hairline. He had a smile that could disarm anyone and now, after a year of working in the area of books and libraries, he had regained his strength from the centuries of being drained in the disappearance of his old job of being the God of Lamplighters.

I sipped on the remains of the milkshake and figured Patty and I needed to order something from Madge pretty soon to keep our strength up. Patty had barely touched her lunch salad as well.

Ben hadn't eaten a thing, even though I offered to buy him something a couple of times.

Patty was sitting beside me, but staring off out the window at a Southwest airliner making an approach into the airport.

"You know," Ben said. "Part of the solution to this might be in how you dealt with these monsters the first time."

"I've been thinking the same thing," I said. "But nothing we did back then seems to matter much this time around. At least not until we find their home and if they are being controlled."

Patty nodded to that.

"So I heard," Ben said, "that you two met fighting these slots. Is that right?"

Patty nodded and smiled, touching my leg, which always calmed me and excited me in a wonderful way, and this touch was no exception.

"We met slightly before we started working on beating the Slots," I said, smiling and putting my hand over Patty's hand on my leg, "but yes, it was the event that pulled us together."

"So tell me about the meeting," Ben said. "I'm becoming sort of the unofficial historian for the gods, and since you two and your team have saved us all a number of times, it seems logical for me to know how all this started."

I honestly didn't know what to say. I wasn't sure how this would help us find the ghost slots, but at this point I trusted Ben and he seemed to think it might be a good use of our time.

Besides, there wasn't one damn thing I could think to do otherwise at the moment.

"You tell your side, first," Poker Boy," Ben said. "Then Patty, you can tell your side of the event."

"The first meeting?" I asked, glancing at Patty. "I honestly can't see how this will help."

"The first meeting," Ben said. "If it doesn't trigger something, then at least it will kill some time here while we wait."

I nodded and sat back. With Patty's hand on my leg, I let myself remember that first meeting with the woman of my life.

CHAPTER THREE
The Memory of that First Meeting

I LOVE CASINOS. Always have.

I mean I truly love them, like some people enjoy sitting beside a calm mountain lake. Walking into a casino, it feels like I've stepped on an ocean beach on a warm evening with no wind, combined with the at-home feel of sitting by a fire, under a nice reading light, with a warm drink and a good book.

I admit, casinos are loud, with both machine and people noises, and are designed by experts to take a person's money. Yet every time I step through the door into a casino, either in Vegas, Atlantic City, or in Timbuck-six North Dakota, I know I am home, that I am safe, that I am in control of my surroundings.

As I stepped through the side door of the Horseshoe that day ten years ago, I walked right into the center of at least forty poker tables. I knew at once I had once again found my own little slice of heaven.

I could feel the power flowing through me. My muscles, tense and tight from the long plane and cab ride, relaxed as if rubbed by a Swedish hot-rub expert.

Now remember, at that point I had only been in the superhero ranks for less than five years, and Stan had pretty much let me go on my own after a little talk or two. So green doesn't begin to describe me when it comes to all this god stuff. I'm still that way.

Ben waved for me to continue, so I did.

I remember that day stopping and just taking a deep breath of the smoke-tainted air of the old casino, filling my lungs with the poisons that killed others, but gave me strength.

Stopping just inside a casino front door was a habit of mine. Still is when I have time.

That day I remember clearly that everything around me looked like a standard day in casino world. And I had no sense that anything was off.

On my right were some of the live poker games, on my left the overflow part of the tournament area, now with all the tables empty. The main desk for the hotel was beyond all the tables, and I had to get there by sort of following the yellow brick road of the pattern on the carpet, through the tables, down between the railings along the live poker tables, and then through the ropes in the open area in front of the hotel desk.

Those ropes that guard the front desks of most hotels and ticket counters in airports always make me feel like a cow being herded to the guy with the hammer who would hit me, put me out of my misery, and turn my body into prime rib and flank steaks. I'm fairly certain some hotels have almost done that to me in the past.

There wasn't anyone waiting in line to check in at that moment. I remember clearly thinking that maybe I could avoid the ropes altogether and just go for the hammer.

I remember putting my head down and moving toward the front desk, pulling my suitcase behind me like a bad child, following the pattern on the carpet, hoping I could get checked in quickly and then take a nap.

I was there for the World Series of Poker which at that point was still held at Binion's Horseshoe Casino. I remember I somehow made it all the way to the front desk without stopping.

"Good afternoon, sir," I remember the woman behind the front desk saying as I stepped up to the polished wood counter.

I remember looking up and honestly, from that point things get a little fuzzy. It was Patty. I remember her smile actually included her brown eyes as she leaned forward a little. And what eyes they are.

"Thank you," Patty said and squeezed my hand.

Ben motioned that I continue and I did.

I think I remember having an out-of-body experience as I studied her eyes.

I knew I could stare into those eyes forever, but I knew I shouldn't.

Yet I remember wanting to.

I remember floating there, arguing with myself, until I finally returned to my body.

"Checking in," I remember that I managed to say, even though my throat was suddenly dry.

"Here for the tournament?" she asked me in return.

I remember saying I was and asking if it was that obvious?

"Poker players do have a look about them," she said to me.

I was in lust with Miss Brown-eyes behind the front desk. I wouldn't learn her name was Patty until later that day.

I gave her one of my many false travel names.

After a moment she said, "Here is your key," and slid the paper packet with the plastic key toward me. I reached for it and her hand brushed mine.

I remember seeing stars!

She wished me, I think, good luck with the tournament, and I thanked her somehow, I think.

Then I turned and tripped over my luggage.

I managed to miss getting tangled in the front desk rope maze as I fell.

That floor may have been carpeted, but I remember it was still hard, and it still hurt.

I remember she leaned over the desk and looked down at me like an angel, the light behind her head giving her a halo, and asked if I was all right.

I thought of staying down, staring at her until she floated over to help me up, then thought better of it.

I sprang to my feet and I somehow managed to not sprint for the elevators.

I looked at Ben and Patty and shrugged. "My side of that first meeting."

Patty squeezed my leg. "You were so cute."

"Falling down was cute?" I asked.

"It was," she said, smiling at me with that same smile I had come to love for ten years.

"So, Patty," Ben said, "tell me your side of what happened."

I looked at her because I realized that in ten years I had never heard her side of that story.

"I knew Poker Boy was coming in for the tournament," Patty said. "And I spotted you at once when you came through the door and stopped. I thought you were cute before you did the dive over the luggage."

"You did?" I asked, stunned.

"Of course," she said, again squeezing my leg. "I had heard a few things about how you had saved some people and a few dogs and stopped Stan from losing his job and all that. So I wanted to meet you."

"Did you know about the Slots of Saturn at that point?" Ben asked Patty.

Patty nodded, which stunned me.

"My boss, Bernice, the God of Hospitality, had been dealing with the missing persons reports all over town. She and I both had a hunch we were dealing with ghost slots, but I honestly didn't want to believe it. None of us did at that point. It was better to think of a more realistic reason than something like ghost slots."

Ben nodded.

I just sat there, surprised.

"So when did you realize you were actually dealing with ghost slots?"

Patty looked at me. "When you and I saw them on the security tape take a customer from the Binion's gaming floor."

I nodded. "That's a memory I'm not going to soon forget."

In fact, just the memory of it right now had me sweating a little.

CHAPTER FOUR
Another Trip to Find a Clue in the Past

BEN ASKED US a few more questions about that second meeting and why we took Samantha, the blind wife of the man who was taken by the slots from Binion's, out of the hotel and to Madge's Diner.

That decision had started our regular meetings for years in the diner and then the design of this office when I built it two years ago.

Going to Madge's had been Patty's idea and my idea to bring in Screamer to help.

Ben walked us all the way through the entire events of that first battle, how we found the slots in the old Standard Slots Graveyard warehouse and how we rescued the people from inside the slots.

Then he asked a very simple question, one that I had a hunch he had been working to for the entire last half hour. "So when was the last time you saw the ghost slots?"

"I remember it clearly," I said. "It was hot, middle of the afternoon."

"A Tuesday," Patty said. "With Screamer, we watched as the two hauling men and two men from Standard Slots hauled the big monster out of the warehouse and craned it up onto a flatbed truck."

"They covered it with tarps and tied it down," I said. "We stood and talked to the Standard men as the two haulers left with it on the back of their truck, headed supposedly to the crusher out at the wrecking yard to the east of town."

Then it dawned on me what I had said. We had a trail, but a ten-year-old trail.

"The truck drivers kept the machine, didn't they?" I said to Ben. "We need to find them and where they kept it the last ten years, or who they sold it to, and we'll have our home for the machines."

I turned to Patty. "You remember the name of the trucking company by any chance? It had a logo on the door."

"Steven's Hauling," Patty said without hesitation.

Damn her memory never ceased to amaze me.

I grabbed my cell phone and dialed The Bookkeeper. Of all the people I knew, he was the best with computers and the internet and research than anyone.

"Still no schedule yet," the Bookkeeper said when he answered the phone.

"Can you trace Steven's Hauling?" I asked. "They picked up the slots ten years ago from the old graveyard warehouse."

"Call you right back," he said.

I hung up and then said, "Stan, we might have a lead."

A moment later Stan appeared with Screamer.

"We're tracking the company that hauled away the slots," I said to him.

"We were trying to find that information out," Stan said, "but the Standard Warehouse Records were long gone. How did you figure it out just sitting here?"

"A short trip down memory lane for Ben," I said, "and Patty's great memory of the name on the truck. Steven's Hauling. I got the Bookkeeper tracing it."

My phone rang.

I answered it and the Bookkeeper said, "Steven's Hauling has been out of business since 2010 when one of their trucks wrecked on the way to LA, killing both of the brothers who owned the company and did all the work of hauling off the slots back ten years ago. Three days after hauling the slots from the warehouse, they deposited three thousand in cash into their bank account that they didn't account for. That was about the going rate for an old set of slots like that back then."

"Nothing else?" I asked.

"All the company records were destroyed in 2012. Now, I'm going back to trying to figure out where these monsters are going to land next."

With that he hung up.

I looked at Patty and Ben and Stan and Screamer. "Dead end. No record of who they sold it to and the brothers who owned and worked the company are dead and all records destroyed."

"And more bad news," Screamer said. "We've got twelve missing so far."

"That the police know about," Stan said.

All I could do was take a deep breath and just wonder what in the world we were going to do to stop this.

Again.

Can't Get Enough of Poker Boy?
These stories and more are available at your favorite booksellers.

CHAPTER FIVE
Got Them!

PATTY AND I were just about to jump to her apartment, change clothes, and head out for a quiet dinner so we could think when Screamer got a call.

He listened for a moment, then said, "Be right there."

He slipped the phone back into his pocket and said, "Slots of Saturn are in Binion's. Same spot as ten years ago. Police have them surrounded, so no unsuspecting customer is going to jump them at the moment."

Instead of teleporting into a dead camera area, it was just as easy for us to head down through Madge's Diner entrance to my office, out the front door, and across the street to Binion's.

The three slot machines that had haunted my dreams for ten years were there, right where Patty and I had seen them on the security tape all those years ago.

And they looked exactly the same. Exactly.

Bright colors, the images of Saturn and the rings cutting across all three machines, three wooden chairs attached in front of them.

My nightmare had returned in bright, living color.

They were pulsing, dim to bright, every second or so, and I could sense the pull they were putting on people around them, including the police.

Including me.

They were hungry and if they didn't find a victim soon, they might jump.

And when they did, we needed to somehow trace them.

I dropped us all out of time, freezing everything around us. I loved that super-power almost as much as I loved the ability to teleport. All I had actually done was take me and Patty and Ben and Screamer and Stan between instants of time.

But all the casino sounds and the sounds coming from Fremont Street stopped instantly. Also, I could thankfully no longer feel the pull from the slots.

"That thing feels like it's about to jump," I said.

Stan nodded and an instant later Laverne appeared wearing her most distinct black power business suit and her hair pulled back tight. A different look than the last time she had been in my office.

"Got any ideas?" she said, staring at the slots.

"It's about to jump, even if it doesn't get fed," I said. "Do we have anyone who can trace that amount of energy through time and space to figure out where it goes?"

There was a long moment of silence inside an already deadly quiet time bubble.

Then Screamer looked at me, then Stan, and Lady Luck. "Is that machine pouring out a lot of energy?"

"It is," Lady Luck said. "And the energy feels very much human, so like the last time, the thing is being powered by the people inside it."

Screamer then said something that surprised me. "We need Sherri here."

Now Sherri was one of Lady Luck's four daughters and Screamer's wife. They had been separated for some time, a couple of decades from what I understood. But Screamer and Sherri had been working slowly to try to figure out a way to be together. I always knew when he and

Sherri had spent time together because he came back smiling.

But at the moment Sherri, who was a superhero, was tending bar in Reno and working for the Gods of Food and Beverage.

She had offered to be part of the team, but until this moment, none of us ever thought to get her involved in any problem.

"Why Sherri?" Lady Luck said a moment before I could.

"She's developed in the last year or so an ability to sense and follow energy," Screamer said. "She can trace a person's energy through a building hours after they walked through it. I think she might be able to trace those monsters, since it's powered by human energy."

Screamer pointed to the frozen ghost slots.

"Didn't know that," Lady Luck said, nodding. "Interesting new type of super-power. Worth a shot. Hold this time bubble and we'll go get her."

Screamer and Lady Luck vanished.

"Did you know Sherri could do that?" I asked both Stan and Patty and Ben.

All of them shook their heads.

"Might be a good power to add into the mix at times," Patty said.

"We shall see," I said, nodding. But I agreed with her. I could think of a couple times that might have been very handy.

An instant later Lady Luck, Screamer, and Sherri appeared.

Sherri was wearing basically the same thing she had on the first time I had met her. Tan slacks, white blouse, and an Eldorado bar apron. She had her long, pitch-black hair pulled back tight, which just accented her stunning beauty.

She and Screamer were holding hands, so I was pretty sure he had transferred to her what was happening. And all the background that had happened ten years ago. He could do that with a touch, let her see inside his head what was happening.

As they appeared, she stepped forward, staring at the Slots of Saturn. "So these are the ghost slots you three defeated ten years ago?"

"They are," Screamer said. "Same damn ones exactly."

"Let's see if I can trace them or not," she said. "Drop the time bubble."

I did as she asked and the sounds of the casino crashed back in around us.

Instantly the wave of energy powered over us from the pulsing slots.

Sherri staggered back into Screamer's arms and collapsed as the slots pulsed faster and faster and faster and then vanished, leaving a newer bunch of slots in its place.

I glanced back at Sherri.

She was out cold and both Screamer and Lady Luck were hovering over her.

A moment later all three of them vanished.

"I'll find out how she's doing," Stan said, and vanished as well, leaving me and Ben and Patty just standing there.

"I think I need a rest," Ben said. "I'll catch up with everyone later."

He vanished.

I looked around at the cops and the people who had been watching all this. And watching all of us just vanish out of thin air. I had no idea how anyone was going to explain all this, or if they would even try, but right at that moment I didn't care.

I jumped Patty and me back to the bedroom of her apartment and stretched out on the bed, not even bothering to take off my leather coat. I used my hat to shade my eyes from what little light was coming around the long drapes pulled closed over the window.

Patty stretched out beside me and took my hand.

"We'll figure it out," she said softly.

I just wished I believed her, because if we didn't, a lot of people were going to die a very ugly death inside a very nasty machine.

CHAPTER SIX
A Nightmare

I DOZED, LYING there on the bed.

In the dream, I was back in that old Standard Warehouse, and Patty and I and Screamer were madly trying to save people as the big machine spit them out, one per second.

Patty had slowed down time just enough that, as the people appeared, Screamer could shove them out of the way onto a big tarp. It had taken us a couple hours to get everyone out that way, with a few problems, but we had done it.

And then the memory dream turned to a nightmare as the ghosts of the people we had saved just wandered the old warehouse full of dead slot machines, not knowing where to go.

And no one would believe they were there.

I woke up with a jerk, sweating.

Patty had gone into the bathroom and was taking a shower.

I lay there, letting my heart slow down, trying to figure out what that dream was all about.

And coming up with nothing.

Ghost slots. Ghost people. That made no sense at all.

Then my cell phone rang. "Sherri's fine," Screamer said. "Meet in your office in an hour for dinner?"

"We'll be there," I said.

I took off my coat and hat and then the rest of my clothes. The nightmare had caused me to sweat right through them.

I headed into the bathroom and crawled into the large shower with Patty, who kissed me, then climbed out.

"What fun is that?" I asked, teasing her, even though I had no intention of fooling around.

"Lot of time for fun when we find those damn machines," she said. "And hurry up, I've got an idea I want to check out."

"Sherri is all right," I said as the cool water rinsed over me, chasing some of the nightmare away. "We're meeting in the office in an hour for dinner."

"Perfect," Patty said, heading out to get dressed.

Twenty minutes later I jumped us across town to a secluded spot near the front gate of an old wrecking yard.

The heat from the desert slammed in on us like a hammer. It always seemed hot in the city, but out in the desert, it always felt worse. And jumping from a comfortable air-conditioned apartment into the direct sun and heat wasn't fun. Especially wearing a black leather coat.

I looked around to make sure we hadn't been spotted. There was no one to see us. The place was acres of dead cars in a small valley to the east of Las Vegas, hidden from sight from just about anything. Sitting in long rows, the old and wrecked cars seemed to just be waiting patiently to be picked apart by car enthusiasts like vultures over dried bones.

A wooden building just inside the open chain-link gate served as an office. They were clearly open. Beyond the office was a huge machine that was in the process of crushing a car, making a noise I didn't want to really listen to for very long. At least not without some great earplugs.

We headed up the dusty gravel road and then into the wooden building that looked like it hadn't been painted since the area was settled.

The door creaked as we went in and a bell rang, as if the door creaking wasn't enough to shout that someone had entered. The cool insides of the office felt like I had dipped my face into a cold drink. We were greeted by an elderly woman who had to be in her seventies. She had on a nametag that read, "Denise" that looked like she was attending a convention more than working in a dusty office in the middle of nowhere.

The place smelled of auto parts and oil and grease, and there were pictures of racing cars on the walls and a large glass case full of trophies, some of which looked to be fifty years old. Some of the pictures jammed all over the walls were clearly of Denise in much younger and thinner days.

"What can I do for you kids?" Denise asked as she climbed to her feet and headed toward us from her cluttered desk.

"We're wondering if your smashing records still go back ten years," Patty asked, giving Denise her best smile and charm that was part of her superpower at front desks.

Patty could calm the most angry customer with a wave of energy and a smile. I could feel the waves of it coming off of her now.

"Oh, sure, dear," Denise said, her voice sounding like a grandmother's voice right out of the movies. "We have records back for forty years since we bought the Big Bully, as we call the noisy old thing."

"Any chance you might have records of crushing an antique three-chair set of slots ten years ago, almost to the day, give or take a few?"

"Let me check," Denise said.

She went to some huge metal filing cabinets that lined the back wall and stretched down one side of a hallway that led to a back office and bathroom.

I wasn't sure exactly what Patty was thinking, because if the slots never arrived here, we were still at the same spot. But I agreed with this search just to make sure they hadn't arrived here and then were sold from here.

Denise pulled open one drawer with a bang and thumbed through a few files for a moment, then checked a few more, and pulled one file, shaking her head.

"We only crushed one slot grouping that entire year," Denise said. "I remember they were really nice-looking old slots owned by Standard, but the guys from the shipping company insisted they help us put them into Big Bully themselves to make sure they were destroyed. Something about them being haunted. It's in the notes here."

Denise shook her head again. "Can you believe haunted slots?"

Neither of us said a thing. I wasn't sure what I believed any more.

Then Denise slipped the manilla file folder across the counter toward Patty.

Patty looked at it and gasped.

I couldn't believe what I was seeing either.

Someone had taken a color Polaroid of the Slots of Saturn half crushed by two huge metal crushing arms of a big machine.

"We take a picture of everything we crush as it's being crushed," Denise said. "That way we're never accused of double-dipping like some crushing yards."

We said nothing. I was too stunned to say anything.

"That what you were looking for?" Denise asked. "Almost ten years to the day as you said."

"That's perfect, thanks," Patty said, pushing the file back to Denise. "Can you make us a copy of that?"

"Oh, sure," Denise said and took the thin file to a copy machine.

A couple minutes later we walked back out into the heat, Patty holding the copies of the file. The smell of desert and old cars hit me again as we walked down the slight hill on the old gravel road and

through the big gate to get out of sight of anyone in the wrecking yard.

How could the slots have been destroyed?

I had just seen them at Binion's just a short few hours before.

"Are we dealing with real ghost slots this time?" Patty asked, her voice low and soft, as we walked through the heat.

"I honestly don't know," I said, feeling completely helpless as I jumped us back to my office overlooking Las Vegas.

I had no idea how to fight machines.

I really had no idea how to fight ghost machines.

CHAPTER SEVEN
A Silent Dinner

AFTER PATTY PASSED around the record from the wrecking yard and the picture, the dinner started off pretty silent. Stan, Ben, Screamer, and Sherri were there with us.

Screamer and Sherri were staying close and sometimes touching across from me in the booth. Ben sat in the back of the booth, saying little, and Stan sat in a chair at the end of the booth.

Madge came and went with food and drinks, but said little. That was normal for her unless she had some observation and like the rest of us, she didn't seem to have many ideas on this mess.

So finally I asked Sherri what exactly she felt when the machine jumped and knocked her out.

"Like I had grabbed a supercharged electrical fence," she said, shaking her head. "Hurt like hell."

Screamer touched her arm and she smiled slightly. Somehow his power and touch must have eased the memory of the pain some.

"Could you tell what kind of energy it was?" Patty asked.

"Human energy," Sherri said without hesitation. "The same kind of energy I can track long after a person goes by. Only multiplied by factors and focused."

"And any sense of the machine now?" Ben asked.

She shook her head. "Nothing. It just vanished."

"Do you think if it was here, you would be able to sense it?"

"I'm sure of it," she said. "And I think I'll know the instant it comes back anywhere in town."

"Well," I said, nodding to myself. "That's going to help."

And I really believed it might. I wasn't sure how, but knowing when it arrived, even if in a place the police didn't have protected, would help a lot.

Screamer smiled at Sherri. "That's what I said."

"I hope so," Sherri said.

At that point Madge brought everyone dinner. This was not the nice, quiet dinner Patty and I had hoped to have, but there were people's lives at stake. We could always go out to a better dinner on another day.

I had ordered deep-fried shrimp. Patty again had some kind of a salad, only with chicken on it.

We all ate pretty much in silence, and I was almost through my shrimp and baked potato when Lady Luck arrived and pulled up a chair next to Stan, who scooted over to give her room.

"Feeling better?" she asked Sherri.

Sherri nodded. "I am, thanks. Any leads?"

Lady Luck shook her head and a moment later Madge appeared and slid a salad similar to Patty's in front of one of the most powerful gods in the world.

We all went back to eating in silence.

I just kept running down everything I could think of, and I kept coming up blank. Then I remembered the Bookkeeper who had been trying to predict the machines.

"Stan, have you checked with the Bookkeeper?" I asked.

He shook his head. "Just makes him angry when I push him."

"Don't you think he needs to know the machines were destroyed ten years ago?"

Stan nodded and took out his cell phone, standing to move off to talk with the Bookkeeper.

Lady Luck looked at me with that stare of hers again, the one that could melt a normal person and pretty much did to me. I couldn't imagine what it must have been like for her daughters to grow up with that look.

"Destroyed?" Lady Luck asked.

I nodded and Patty took the copies of the file from beside her and handed them to Lady Luck.

"Son of a bitch," Lady Luck said after a moment of looking inside, then handing the file back to Patty.

I didn't know she swore like that.

Then Lady Luck took another forkful of her salad, stuffed it in her mouth, and vanished.

As we all sat there, sort of in shock at Lady Luck swearing, Stan came back over to the table and sat down. "The Bookkeeper was swearing at me when he hung up."

"Mom just did the same thing," Sherri said, shaking her head. "That's not a good thing when Mom swears."

When Mom was Lady Luck, there was no chance in the world I was going to disagree with that.

CHAPTER EIGHT
Another Encounter

TEN MINUTES LATER not a one of us could figure why both Lady Luck and the Bookkeeper were so upset about the machines having been destroyed ten years before.

"There's something none of us know," Stan said, "that they clearly do and don't really want to tell us yet."

I couldn't argue with that, but as a lowly superhero, I was sort of used to either being in the dark, or just flat uninformed. I didn't like it, but I had gotten used to the feeling. It was why I liked having Ben around. He helped me with the history.

I turned to him with that thought. "Any record of anything like this happening before?"

"Nothing," he said. "Nothing even close in thousands of years of my memory."

Suddenly, Sherri tipped forward and grabbed her head.

Screamer instantly held her, clearly working to help her in some fashion, his eyes closed.

After a moment I asked softly, "Need help?"

"Patty," he said.

Patty reached across the booth without hesitation and touched Sherri's arm and then closed her eyes.

At that moment I knew all three of them were linked up for some reason. And I had a hunch I knew what the reason was.

The machines were back in town from wherever they went.

And Screamer and Patty were helping Sherri set up some mental shields against the intense energy.

Finally, after what seemed like a very long time, but must have only been fifteen seconds, Patty sat back and released her touch on Sherri.

"Machines are back at Binion's again," Patty said.

Sherri sat up straight and opened her eyes. They looked a little haunted, but not bad.

"Thanks," she said to Screamer and Patty. "I can deal with them now if I don't get too close."

Screamer's phone rang and he answered it. Then after a moment he said, "Make sure no one goes near them."

"Police still have the area surrounded," Screamer said. "So we won't lose another person this time."

"Think from this distance you might be able to follow the machines this time when they jump?" I asked Sherri.

She nodded. "With Patty and Screamer's help I can try."

Patty slipped out of the booth and slid in on the other side with Sherri and Screamer. I watched from across the expanse of empty plates and used drinking glasses as the three of them got ready.

I felt helpless. But I knew that sometimes a leader of a group was best left observing. I didn't like it, but I knew that to be the case now.

All three of their minds were going to be linked.

"It's powering up to jump," Sherri said.

Screamer held her shoulders and Patty reached over and held onto Sherri's arm.

All three of them closed their eyes, clearly no longer mentally in the booth.

After four or five seconds, all three of them jerked as if shocked. Then they slumped.

I wanted to shout to see if Patty was all right, but somehow I held my panic under control slightly.

Finally Patty opened her eyes, looking at me and smiling at what must have been a panicked look on my face.

"Could you trace them?" Stan asked.

Patty shook her head and took a deep breath.

"We should have been able to follow them," Sherri said, opening her eyes as well and looking at Stan. "Anywhere on the planet. But it was as if the surge shut them off as they vanished."

Screamer nodded agreement and handed Sherri a glass of water.

"We never saw them shut off ten years ago," I said. "So is there any place on this planet you couldn't trace them to?"

"Nowhere," Sherri said, and beside her Screamer again nodded in agreement. He had been inside her head, he knew what she felt and saw as well.

Suddenly Lady Luck was back at the end of the table.

She pulled up a chair, still clearly upset. "You are both right and wrong, daughter. There is no place on this planet you could not have traced them to with your power and the help of your husband and Patty."

"So where are they?" I asked.

"They are on this planet," Lady Luck said, looking at me. "Just not in this timeline."

Lady Luck took a forkful of the salad still sitting in front of her. And before putting it in her mouth she added, "and not in this time period either."

CHAPTER NINE
A Time Headache

I HATED ANY thought of time travel. It always gave me a headache.

And now just mentioning it again felt like it might give me one again.

Patty stood and stretched and then came around and slid back into the booth beside me. She touched me and I could feel she was tired, drained from her experience with Sherri and Screamer.

I focused some energy in her direction through our contact and she smiled, letting the energy in so that she could regain some strength. I liked that about our relationship. Together we were a lot, lot stronger than alone.

Before I could even formulate a question for Lady Luck, Stan's phone rang.

"Bookkeeper," Stan said, and answered the phone without leaving the table.

"Yeah," Stan said. "We know that."

Then he listened for a moment and I watched his face. It wasn't easy to get a read on the God of Poker, but sometimes when Stan wasn't aware, he let down his guard. And this was one of those times.

His eyebrows seemed to creep up his forehead toward his receding hairline as he clearly got news he didn't want to hear.

Then he asked, "How long?"

"Thanks," Stan said after a moment. "Anything else, call me."

He clicked off his cell phone and looked at the silent group around the table.

"We have fourteen hours," Stan said, "to solve this."

"I was afraid of that," Lady Luck said. "That's what Kronos told me as well."

Kronos, the God of Time, was the only one allowed to travel in time. He controlled it and if he thought this was a problem, it really was a problem.

"What happens in twenty-three hours?" Sherri asked.

"This timeline we are in is permanently separated from our original timeline," Stan said.

Lady Luck and Ben were both shaking their heads, clearly understanding what that meant.

And knowing what he meant.

I had no clue. Not one.

And I could tell the other superheroes at the table had no idea what the gods were saying or thinking, since there were blank looks on the faces I could see. I could feel my look was as puzzled as the rest.

"What happens then?" Screamer asked.

"This entire timeline drops into a time loop," Lady Luck said.

"A what?" Screamer asked a moment before I could get out the question.

"Think *Groundhog Day*, the movie," Stan said, "only we won't have a memory of anything repeating."

"This timeline would just repeat the last few days," Lady Luck said flatly, "plus the next fourteen hours over and over and over. We would never know it and never escape."

My stomach clamped up so tight I wasn't sure if I could even swallow. And my lungs seemed to expel every ounce of breath they were holding.

That was the worst kind of jail I could ever imagine.

"How do we know," I asked, afraid of the question, "that we didn't fail and are already in a time loop?"

"We don't," Lady Luck said. "So let's not fail, because I don't want to eat this salad for the rest of eternity."

CHAPTER TEN
A Ticking Clock

AFTER WE ALL sat there for a few long moments in silence, thinking about our possible eternities having dinner together, the same dinner, and not knowing we were doing it, I finally managed to get a thought in my brain and let it come out my mouth.

"What caused this in the first place?"

"You did," Stan said.

"We all did," Lady Luck corrected. "None of us knew. We were just glad Poker Boy and Patty and Screamer saved the gambling industry, remember?"

"I'm not following," I said.

"We saved people the machine had taken from this timeline and just left them in the past," Patty said.

Now I knew that didn't sound good.

Stan nodded. "So to get those same people again, the machine has to jump to another timeline and take the same people again and again and again. Jumping from timeline to timeline. A time loop creating new alternate realities off the same event."

"So we already saved everyone who is in the machine the first time?" I asked.

"You did," Lady Luck said, nodding. "Now we have to save all the rest of us and everyone in this timeline."

"So the main timeline actually got split back ten years ago?" Screamer asked.

Lady Luck nodded.

"So to stop this," I asked. "Will Kronos allow us to go back in time and fix the mistake?"

"He will," Lady Luck said. "I already asked him and he agreed if I went along. We can bring the victims back to the future and that will reset all the timelines."

I could feel my stomach starting to unclamp. "So what's the problem?"

She looked at me. "Do you know which people you saved were from that past time and which were from this time?"

"Oh," Patty said, slumping slightly beside me.

"We don't have a lot of time to figure that out," I said. "We can do that, can't we?"

Lady Luck nodded. "We can, but if we miss one, we're into the time loop and will always miss one."

She was so full of good news I couldn't stand it.

She stood. "I've got some things to set up, and I need to talk with Kronos again."

She vanished.

I took a deep breath and pushed the headache back. We needed to get moving and move fast. I turned to Stan. "Can you get the Bookkeeper on this?"

"He said he would start the computer searches for them when I talked with him. He should have a list for us shortly."

I nodded. "We don't want to trust it, though." I looked at Stan again. "Can you talk with the gods in charge of the police and get a full list of names we rescued?"

"I'll get it," Stan nodded and vanished.

"So what do we do?" Screamer asked.

I sat there staring at the four left around the table that was still covered with our dinner dishes. Then it suddenly dawned on me that we had yet another way of getting information.

We could travel back without actually traveling in time.

"Screamer, when you pushed those people out of the chair, you touched them."

"I did," he said, frowning at me. "Do you really think after ten years that I can remember flashes of who they all were just from touching them for an instant?"

"I do," I said, smiling at my friend. "With help. Whatever we get can work as another check-point to make sure the lists we get are 100% accurate."

"I don't know how I could do that," Screamer said, shaking his head.

"It won't just be you," I said. "Remember, all three of us were hooked up and thus all three of us caught a glimpse of the mind of each person you touched."

"Good point," Patty said, "But I don't think I remember much either."

"I remember us being a little busy," Screamer said.

"But we have a secret weapon."

I looked directly into the wonderful brown eyes of the love of my life. It took her a moment, but then she laughed, clearly understanding what I was getting at.

She smiled at me and then turned to Screamer. "Remember how I slowed the time down so we can get the people out of the chairs?"

Screamer nodded.

"I can slow the time down even more in memory. A lot more."

I looked at Ben, who just smiled at me and nodded his agreement.

"Ben can remember what we all only caught a glimpse of in each person," I said, "if he's linked to us when we go back into the memory."

Screamer nodded slowly. "You know, Poker Boy, that's a hairbrained scheme like most of your schemes, and it just might work."

I was sure hoping it would.

"And what am I going to do?" Sherri asked.

I looked at her and then at Screamer. "Keep all of us calm and focused, since that few hours we spent getting those people out was very traumatic for all of us, and will be hard to relive."

She looked at her husband and nodded. "I can do that."

"Ben," I said, turning to him, "are you going to be able to remember all the details we each see with each person we rescued?"

He laughed. "I promise, I won't miss a detail, no matter how small. But I suggest we do nine at a time, stop, and I relay everything I got to see if it matches what everyone remembers from the experience."

"Very good idea," I said. "That way we won't be totally stressed."

"Oh, we'll be stressed," Patty said. "I never thought I'd have to relive those hours of sheer terror again."

"I didn't either," Screamer said. "I had nightmares for years about bodies materializing inside of each other."

"We got to do this," I said, shuddering at the memory of that exact same nightmare. "And we have to get it right."

"Because if we don't," Screamer said, "we're destined to relive what we are about to try over and over and over inside a time loop."

"That's not a time loop," I said. "That's hell."

"I've been down on a visit to hell," Sherri said. "This would be worse."

Everyone but Screamer looked at her.

I think I had my mouth open.

She looked around and smiled. "What? An old boyfriend is all. You know how kids are."

"Before my time," Screamer said, shaking his head.

CHAPTER ELEVEN
A Second Time Through a Nightmare

WE TOLD MADGE what we were planning and she cleaned off the table and brought us all pads of paper and pens and some fresh glasses of water.

While she was doing that, Sherri and Screamer jumped to her mother to tell her the plan and I called to Stan to come back and I explained the plan to him.

Lady Luck and Stan both thought it was a good idea.

While we were getting set up, Stan got in the list from the Bookkeeper of the names and location his computers told him were the ones from the future we stranded in the past.

I wouldn't let Stan show it to us, since I didn't want what we were about to try to be contaminated in any way.

Stan thought that very smart and agreed. He jumped away to continue to get help from the police on the overall list of names.

So as we all slipped into the booth, we put Screamer in the middle in the back. Sherri was on one side of him and Ben beside her.

Patty was on the other side of Screamer and I was beside her.

Patty and I and Screamer had had our minds together a lot over the years, but this was the first time we had tried it with both Sherri and Ben also in the mix.

"Stay focused on the memory," I said and everyone agreed.

"We start from the first one and go through?" Screamer asked.

"From the first one," I said and he nodded.

Why he had asked about the first one was because the first person out of the machine had been Geneva, a reporter from the *Las Vegas Sun* who we had sent in so that we could communicate with someone inside. She and her boyfriend, a cop friend of mine named Johnny, had developed a very tight mental connection that we used.

I wanted to make sure we didn't get confused in the order and miss anyone.

"Ready for a ride back to hell?" Screamer asked.

Patty and I both nodded.

Sherri took Ben's hand on top of the table and touched Screamer's leg with the other.

Patty touched my leg and then took Screamer's hand on top of the table.

Instantly there were four other people in my head.

I tried to only focus on my memory of that hot day in that graveyard of slot machines.

Patty and Screamer did the same and Sherri sent some waves of calming energy as we were again back in front of those monster machines ten years before.

Ben just felt like a shadow in the distance, watching.

The intense terror I felt overwhelmed me and I could feel Patty's and Screamer's fear as well.

We were standing right in front of the pulsating machines. I was touching Screamer and Patty was holding my hand.

I got the distinct smell of raspberry shampoo, but pushed that thought away and focused on what was about to happen.

Patty had slowed down time and then, slowly, in the chair in front of the right-side slot machine, a woman's body started to materialize seated in the wooden chair.

Screamer reached out when she was complete and shoved her hard out of the way.

I focused on her mind, what was in it, and caught a lot about her and her new relationship with Johnny. More than I thought I could get, actually.

Can't Get Enough of Poker Boy?
These stories and more are available at your favorite booksellers.

The next person, a woman, started to materialize and I remember thinking how close that was and how fast that was happening, even with Patty slowing time.

Scary fast, Patty thought at me. *I had my eyes closed and hadn't realized it was that close. No wonder you and Screamer have nightmares of people materializing together.*

More than you want to know, Screamer thought at her.

As the woman finished materializing, Screamer pushed her hard out of the way and onto the mat beside the chair. She landed in slow motion on top of Geneva.

The woman's mind seemed open to me. I scanned as much as I could in the fraction of a second Screamer was in contact with her. I could see in her memory that when she was taken by the slots, there was a 2004 Mercedes spinning slowly on some progressive slot machine display to her right. And she was thinking she would really love to win that new car.

Casinos didn't give away old cars, so she was from that time, not today.

The next one out was Ben, the man Patty and I had seen taken from Binion's.

We knew he was fine as well.

Back then we had taken two minutes rests between every group of three, but we didn't need to do that in memory, so we jumped over the two minutes and went through the next three people out of the machine, then did that again with three more.

Then both Patty and Sherri broke their connection with Screamer as we planned.

"Wow, you three were terrified," Sherri said. "I'm impressed you managed to save all those people under that kind of stress and fear. And working with untested superpowers as well. Amazing."

"Thanks for keeping us calm this time through," Screamer said and leaned over

and kissed her. "That was a lot better than the first time we had to live that."

I had to agree with him. Sherri was managing to keep the fear in all of us that we felt back then pushed back.

I turned to Ben. "Did you get it all?"

"Every detail," he said. "We start from the first person."

We all grabbed our papers and pens and Ben gave us the first person's full name and when she was born and how she had gotten taken.

We all agreed on the first one, that what he said matched what we saw as well.

He went on to the second woman, then on to Ben, detailing all three out.

Then he went to the next three, and again all three were taken in 2004. That much was clear, without a doubt.

On each person who it was clear was from 2004, I drew a line through their name on my pad.

It wasn't until we got to number eight out of the machine that we found our first person from this present time.

There was no doubt at all with him.

His name was Willie (William) Jamison. He had been taken as the last one from this time period. He had been twenty-one when taken.

"Oh, no," Patty said as Ben described him.

"What?" I asked.

"Remember his face," Patty said. "Do you recognize it?"

"Oh, bloody hell," Screamer said, shaking his head.

I could picture the guy's face and it did look familiar, but darned if I could remember from where.

"He took on the name Ben Williams," Patty said, "back in 2004."

And then it flooded over me. Ben Williams had killed a middle-aged couple in a very brutal and angry fashion in what was called a home invasion. He was found covered in the couple's blood holding their twelve-year-old son. He was sentenced to life in prison and the press said he never showed remorse.

"He was an abused child," Ben said softly. "When he found himself stuck in the past, he had to save his younger self from his own parents."

"And that's why we have alternate realities," Lady Luck said, appearing in front of the booth. "Kronos didn't notice that one forming because it made so little impact, since his parents did nothing and in the main timeline will die not many years from now anyway."

"And the young Willie?" I asked, afraid of the answer.

"He killed himself in foster care at the age of sixteen."

"Keep up the good work," she said, nodding to the silence in the room and then vanishing.

We had one.

We had gone through only nine of over a hundred.

This really was hell. We just had to make sure we didn't miss anyone from this time so that we didn't repeat this hell into eternity.

No pressure.

CHAPTER TWELVE
The Swamp of People's Lives

WE MADE IT through the next nine without finding anyone from our time. Of that I was 100 percent sure. With Patty slowing down even more the moment that Screamer had touched each person, we were all digging into each person's life.

And there was a lot of it I flat didn't want to dig into.

One was a child molester that when we went over it with our pens and paper, both Screamer and I made a note to look up to see if he was still alive.

Others had strange sexual habits that were not illegal, but made me look away. Others were buried in loneliness, others still were using gambling as a way to escape one ugly thing or another in their life. Of the nine, not a one of them was a happy person.

I'm not sure if that was a comment on slot players or just the luck of the draw.

As we finished with the third nine and came back to the present, Madge brought us all milkshakes and big baskets of hot fries. The vanilla milkshake tasted wonderful and the fries were perfect.

I didn't realize how much I needed both.

We again went over each name and it was number twenty-two that had come from today.

Penny Smith was her name. She had been widowed the year before at the age of fifty-four and was using gambling with slots to take her mind off her sorrow of losing the man of her life to cancer. I had no idea what she had done when she discovered she was trapped in the past, and I wasn't sure I wanted to know.

Screamer said the same thing.

Patty and Sherri said nothing.

Ben seemed to never make a comment on the people whose privacy we were invading.

So we had two after going through twenty-seven people.

We found the next one from this time two groups of nine later. Number forty-two.

She was a widower at thirty-five because her husband had been murdered. Actually, it was clear in her mind that she had murdered him for having an affair on her.

She had gotten all his money, played the grieving widow for a year or so, and then moved to Vegas last year.

"We'll deal with her after all this is settled," Screamer said, smiling at me.

I had no doubt he and the police would deal with her just fine. But after seeing the inside of that woman's evil mind, I wanted to help, or at least watch the police arrest her. She had already been plotting on finding her next rich husband when we stranded her in the past.

Beside me, Patty shuddered. "There is true evil out there, isn't there?"

I touched her arm and gave her energy to go on.

She smiled at me and said, "Thanks. Not so sure how I got so lucky to find someone like you."

"Raspberry shampoo," I said.

Screamer snorted and Patty had the decency to blush.

I had a clear memory of being in lust with Patty right from the first time I saw her. But all these trips into the memories of that time were making the fact that I really had fantasies about her and her raspberry soap in a shower, long before we climbed into that first shower together.

I loved that soap then and now.

"Clear your mind, mister," she said, softly smacking my arm. "We have work to do."

And I tried, I really did. But it's raspberry shampoo, after all.

CHAPTER THIRTEEN
Just One Small Problem Named Hank

WE GOT THROUGH all of the people we rescued from the ghost slots and found eleven.

We were all convinced there were only the eleven. I'm not a betting man, but I would have bet that was it. Of course, we were betting our entire lives and all the lives in this timeline that we were right.

We were also all exhausted, completely and totally.

"All right, Stan," I said into the air and he appeared.

"Ready for the Bookkeeper's list?" he asked.

"We are," I said.

Lady Luck appeared and sat at the end of the table with Stan. She grabbed one of the cold fries and started biting on it.

I had a master list in front of me and Patty, so I said, "Read off your names."

Lady Luck seemed to have a list as well and was following along.

He did, and I put a check beside each name that agreed with our list.

And then he read the name Hank Carson.

No Hank Carson on our list.

We all looked up at him and he clearly read our expressions.

"Oh, oh," he said.

"Hank's on my list as well," Lady Luck said. "Kronos and I put it together from studying time stream shifts over the last ten years."

I looked at Patty, then at Ben.

"No Hank Carson came out of the machine," I said.

Stan nodded and went on with the list. Everything agreed except that one name.

"How many people are between the two names we agree on?" Stan asked.

"Thirteen," Ben said. "Is Hank Carson a man or a woman?"

"A man," Lady Luck said.

"Then only four men are candidates," he said.

I flipped back through my notes to the four he was talking about and looked at them again.

All five of us did the same. I remembered all four men clearly. All had clearly been from 2004.

After a moment I looked up. "We go back. Look for anything out of place, dig deeper into these four."

Screamer nodded and said, "Ready."

Sherri took Ben's hand, Patty put her hand on my leg.

I took Screamer's hand and Sherri touched his leg.

And once again we were back in front of those damn evil machines.

Concentrate, Ben thought at us.

The first man came out and Screamer pushed him aside. But as he did, Patty slowed down time and we all dove into the poor man's mind.

After what seemed like far too long inside a stranger's head and looking into his very personal thoughts and actions, Screamer thought to us, *He's clean.*

We went on to the next guy.

Same.

And the next guy.

Same.

And the final guy.

Same.

There was no doubt, all four of them were taken by the slots in 2004.

Screamer broke the connection and we all turned to look at Stan and Lady Luck.

"No Hank Carson?" Stan asked.

"No Hank Carson," I said.

"Damn it," Lady Luck said again as she stood. "What the hell is going on here?"

And with that she vanished.

"I hate it when Mom swears," Sherri said, shaking her head and looking at her notes. "Things tend to turn ugly when that happens."

I could sure understand that. Never wanted to get Lady Luck mad. Something about that just seemed really, really dangerous.

I looked over at Stan. "How many hours do we have left?"

"Ten," he said.

Ten hours to save everyone in the world from being trapped in a nasty time loop. No wonder it was strictly against the rules to time travel. This kind of stuff was just far, far too dangerous.

CHAPTER FOURTEEN
Looking for Hank in
All the Wrong Places

THE MOMENT LADY Luck vanished, Stan got back onto the phone with the Bookkeeper and gave him the name of Hank Carson. "We need every detail about the guy, right down to his shoe size," Stan said.

He listened to the Bookkeeper say something for a moment, nodded and then hung up without saying another word.

"He'll have it all within a half hour," Stan said, sitting back down at the table.

Around us the sky was starting to darken and now the planes coming into the airport had lights on. Pretty soon, stretched out below my invisible floating office, the lights of Las Vegas would be on and in full glory. Normally, I loved looking at those lights from here, but right now I didn't feel much like looking at anything except my hands.

Finally, I took a deep breath, put my hand on Patty's arm, and looked at the group. "So if we didn't pull Hank Carson out of that machine, why are both Kronos and the Bookkeeper showing that he was there and part of what caused this alternate timeline?"

I looked around at my team. "I'm open for theories or even wild speculation."

Screamer shrugged. "He got with one of the survivors and discovered information about the future and used it, thus causing Kronos and the Bookkeeper both to pick up the disruptions he caused."

I nodded. I had figured as much. So if we pulled the others from the past and brought them back to the present, they would never hook up with Hank and thus that would take care of him.

But that was taking a horrible gamble I didn't want to take.

And it honestly didn't feel right to me. My little voice I trusted in poker said that wasn't the right way to go.

"A second option," Sherri said, "is that he's some sort of time traveler that used the trips by the Slots of Saturn to cover his tracks from Kronos."

"There are time travelers?" I asked, feeling stunned.

Sherri nodded. "Mostly from the distant future, but Kronos and his teams keep them out of these times for just this reason."

I glanced at Stan and he was nodding.

"If that's the case, it's out of our hands," I said.

Everyone around the table agreed. If that was the case, that was a problem for Kronos and Laverne.

I looked at everyone. "Any more options, suggestions, or just flat wild theories?"

"The first one seems the most logical," Ben said.

"But that seems like something that Kronos and the Bookkeeper would have taken into account," I said. "All of these people will have talked to some people at one point or another."

"I agree," Screamer said.

"There's something we're missing," I said.

So once again we all sat there in silence.

At that moment, Madge appeared from the diner with a tray of milkshakes. "I can hear all of you thinking clear downstairs," she said, "so thought I would bring some thinking food."

She also had a couple of baskets of hot fries.

I watched as Patty took one, then dropped it and sucked on her thumb.

"Hot out of the fryer," Madge said. "Sorry, should have warned you."

Something just dinged at me really hard.

It was that poker sense of mine that dinged like a little alarm bell to tell me I was missing a detail that was right in front of me.

Patty inspected her thumb for a moment, then put it against the cold glass of the vanilla milkshake in front of us.

Again the little dinger in my head dinged again, like an annoying timer I needed to shut off but couldn't find.

Then it dawned on me what I was seeing.

Patty's thumb.

Hitchhiker.

Someone hadn't been taken inside the slot machines, but had hitchhiked back in time on them.

"Thank you, Madge," I said, sucking on the milkshake so hard it gave me an ice cream headache. "You gave us the answer."

"I did?" she asked, looking puzzled and everyone else looked at me in the same way.

"Patty," I said, "show everyone your burnt thumb."

"It's not really burnt," she said.

"Show them," I said, smiling at her. She did.

"Now, with your thumb sticking out, make a fist."

She did.

"Of course," Stan said, laughing. "Damn it, Poker Boy, how do you make these weird connections?"

"What connections?" Screamer asked. "Missed me."

Patty was smiling at me and as she did, she stuck out her thumb again over the middle of the table, moving it from left to right as she said, "Going my way, mister?"

"Hitchhiker?" Screamer asked.

Sherri laughed and Ben just nodded.

"We know who we got out of the machine," I said.

"Not who rode on the back of the machine into the past," Stan said.

"Exactly," I said. "I know I never thought of looking around behind those machines."

"I didn't either," Patty said.

"But we have one problem," Stan said. "We don't know exactly when he took that trip back. He wasn't in any of the police reports of those rescued."

"So he went back with one of the first ones," Patty said, "and when the machine jumped again, he got out of the warehouse."

I could feel my stomach tightening up again. Those machines had been operating for almost a week before we got to the warehouse. Hank could have found himself in that warehouse at any point over that week and we wouldn't know when.

Ben looked at me and said, "We have only ten hours to figure out when he arrived there and get him before he gets out of that warehouse. And then get the other eleven back to our time as well."

"If that is how he got back there," Screamer said. "Remember, our first option is the most logical, that he met someone from the future and was influenced by them."

I shook my head. "That doesn't feel right. The Bookkeeper would have spotted that. No, I think Hank rode along without meaning to. Not sure why I know that, but just a sense. Now we just have to figure out how."

And with that, again the silence filled the booth and my office overlooking the beautiful city of Las Vegas as the sun slowly set over the western hills.

CHAPTER FIFTEEN
Once More into the Nightmare

"SO HOW DO we find out when he rode back on the machines?" Sherri asked.

I looked at her and then asked the next logical question. "How could someone ride along and not be in the machine?"

"Touching it from the back," Screamer said.

Beside me, Patty shook her head. "Slot machines in this modern time are almost impossible to get close to from the back, unless he was a maintenance worker or a slot tech. Sitting in one of the other chairs is the most logical thing to have happened."

I couldn't believe I had forgotten that the machine was actually three slot machines.

With three wooden chairs attached.

It was only the machine on the right side that had come alive and had taken all our focus, but the other two machines rode along because it was a three-machine unit.

"Of course," I said. "We go back again, focus only on the moment the person from this time period was pulled into the machine to see if anyone was sitting next to them."

"And once we spot him," Screamer said, "we'll have a general timeline."

"I agree," Ben said. "We can figure out exactly when the two people on either side from that time were pulled through. That should narrow the time down to a few hours."

"So we go back to the nightmare and inside the heads of the eleven people taken from this time."

Everyone nodded. But clearly none of them were any happier with the idea than I was.

"I'll tell Lady Luck what you are doing," Stan said, and vanished.

Screamer was still sitting in the middle, with Patty on one side and me on the other.

"One more time?" I asked.

"Do we have a choice?" Screamer asked.

"Not that I can think of," I said.

"Then one more time."

Again, we scooted together in the booth and all touched so that our minds were all hooked up.

I thought at everyone, *Focus at the first person from our time and the moment they were at the machine.*

We did just that.

And once again I was back in that warehouse, with the feeling of panic and fear crawling all over me like a nest of spiders. Sherri instantly calmed all of us down.

Thanks, Patti thought.

Again, with Sherri keeping us calm, I could actually think and get out of the panic I felt back ten years ago as we fought to save over a hundred people from those machines.

We were again in slow motion as Patty had slowed time down, and we were back in our own memories. Then the woman from our time slowly appeared, being spit out by the machine like a bad coin, and Screamer pushed her out of the chair.

Patty slowed the moment down even more so that we could see into the poor woman's mind and see if there happened to be anyone around her that she noticed when she sat at the slots.

No one.

She was the only one in the chairs when the machine took her, and there was no way anyone could get in behind the old slots either, since they were against a wall.

One down, I thought at everyone.

We went through three more people from our time before we found what we were looking for.

The man named Jeffrey Johns, number sixty-four in the list of people we had rescued from the machine. He had just sat down in the chair when the machine was back at Binion's in this time period.

Suddenly, beside him, another man slid into the left seat.

There was a clear thought of annoyance from Jeffrey because he had been thinking of playing all three slot machines at the same time. Then he was pulled into the machine and into the past.

I got a clear image of the man who sat down in the left chair. Balding head, overweight, Bermuda shorts, and a Hawaiian shirt of loud blues and oranges.

I have a hunch that's him, I thought at everyone.

We check all eleven, Ben thought clearly.

I agreed.

And we did, and that was the only hitchhiker we found from our time back into the past.

Screamer cut the connection and we all moved back into our positions at the booth. Stan had returned and he

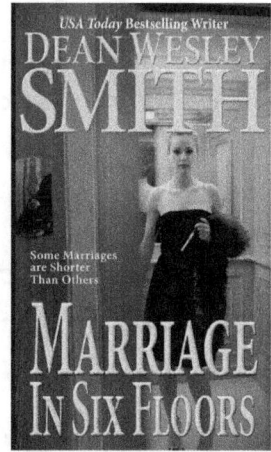

and Madge were there, waiting for us to return from the nightmare of the past that we had been exploring in our minds.

"We found him," I said, smiling.

Ben quickly looked through his notes. "He arrived in 2004 somewhere in an eight-hour-period of time."

"Great job," Stan said. "Poker Boy, call the Bookkeeper and see if he can narrow the time down some. I'll tell Lady Luck so she can work with Kronos."

Then he vanished.

I grabbed my phone and quickly told the Bookkeeper what we had found and he said simply, "I'll be back with you in twenty minutes."

"So how long did that take?" I asked.

I was known for not wearing a watch or being able to keep track of time that well. Yet in this countdown, we had to keep track.

"We have just under nine hours to stop the time loop from setting," Ben said.

My heart sank and I could feel what energy I had left sort of draining out of me. And as it did, it was as if I could suddenly hear a huge clock ticking.

Just ticking in the distance.

On and on and on.

Slowly getting louder and taunting me with every tick of the clock.

CHAPTER SIXTEEN
Planning the Past

PATTY AND I sat there sipping our vanilla milkshake. It had partially melted while we were on that last visit into our shared nightmare, but it was still good. And neither of us cared. We were both just trying to get some energy for whatever came next.

The fries were still just warm enough to eat, so we munched on a few of those as well.

I could tell from Patty's hand on mine that she had been drained by helping Sherri and slowing time even more when we were back in time.

Suddenly, across from us, Sherri, who had been sitting, mostly staring at her milkshake, grabbed her head and bent over in pain.

Screamer instantly had his arm around her and Patty leaned across the table and touched her as well.

I couldn't believe it. The damn slot machines were back again.

I stared at the three of them, wishing I could do something to help.

Stan just sat there staring as well. If a god was helpless, what could I expect to do?

After a moment, Sherri opened her eyes and sat up. Patty leaned back next to me and through the touch in our shoulders I tried to feed her some energy.

"Where are they?" I asked, afraid of the answer.

"A rundown casino out on the old highway," Patty said. "The Golden Jackpot Casino."

"We don't have police on that one," Stan said.

Instantly he and I both jumped to the old casino.

The energy of the evil slot machines pulsed over me like a wave of desire, working to draw me in with the promise of richness and fun, all for a nickel.

An overweight, middle-aged woman, with dyed-brown hair piled far too high for even the 1960s, was headed for the deadly machine. She had on skin-tight green

Capri pants that from the back should have had a warning sign attached that told a person to never look. She had a plastic bucket of coins tucked against her left breast and was about five steps from the machine.

Another, even heavier and shorter middle-aged woman dressed in even tighter brown Capri pants was one step behind her.

That was a sight I was never going to get out of my mind, and if it hadn't been for the pulsing Slots of Saturn machines beyond them, I would have turned away.

Stan and I both jumped again, appearing in front of the women.

We acted like security guards, both holding our hands up for them to stop.

Both women did stop, shocked expressions showing through the layers of makeup coating their faces.

Before they could ask where we came from, Stan said. "These machines are broken." His voice echoed through the casino like only a god can make a voice echo.

"They look fine to me," the first woman said, looking past us both. "I love old slot machines."

"Reminds her of her dearly-departed husband," the other woman said, somehow smiling without cracking the layers of makeup.

"He never had a crank like that one," the first woman said, pointing to the long handle with the black nob on the side of the machine.

Both of them laughed.

I shuddered.

"Yeah, you could wish," the second woman said to her friend, and again they laughed.

Behind me I could feel the intense pull of the machines, demanding that someone sit down and feed them.

In front of me were two women who really did belong in the past, but a past far before 2004.

"What can one pull hurt?" the first woman asked, giving Stan a smile that I swore should have broken a couple of layers of caked-on makeup. Her teeth were yellow from too many cigarettes.

"More than you know," Stan said.

He waved his hands at the two women and they vanished.

"Where did you send them?" I asked, looking around to make sure no one had gotten in behind us.

"To the buffet, paid lunch," he said.

"Yeah, that's what they needed," I said, shaking my head.

We spread out a little and for the next three minutes we stood there, backs to the machines, telling people the slots were damaged, as the power of the slots drew people toward them.

Finally, the machines started pulsing bright to dim and then back, more and more, faster and faster, until finally with a flash they jumped back to the warehouse in the past.

They had left empty.

Around us the old casino went on, an occasional bell going off, an occasional yell from a drunk at one of the gaming tables. Without the pulsing energy of the old slot machines, the casino suddenly felt worn and tired. And it smelled of old cigarettes and spilled whiskey on the worn blue carpet.

"Lucky we had Sherri to tell us the slots were here again," I said.

He nodded. "But while you are in the past, she needs to stay here to keep watch."

"I agree," I said.

We both jumped back to my office where Sherri looked like she was just recovering from the jolt of the machine's last jump.

And Patty looked even more tired than before.

I just hoped that at some point this would be over and Patty could rest.

Not that I worried about her or anything.

CHAPTER SEVENTEEN
The Plan

WE KNEW THAT the other eleven people from the future all came back out of the slot machine in just over an hour period as we rescued everyone. We knew that time exactly.

And we knew who they were and what they looked like, so we could intercept them on the way out of the warehouse to the police that we had stationed outside that first time.

But Hank had arrived in a window that the Bookkeeper could only knock down to four hours.

Four hours to find him and get him back, a couple hours to get everyone else back.

Six hours.

We had eight hours until the time loop locked in and trapped us forever. And not even Kronos, the God of Time, could save us.

That was cutting it very close.

Too close for my tastes.

Laverne appeared and nodded to Stan, then to her daughter, then to me as she sat down. She was now dressed in casual clothes. Jeans and a tan sweatshirt that said, "Believe It" on the front.

"Great job stopping yet another one," she said.

"Sherri knew where it came in," I said. "Stan and I just stood guard."

Laverne nodded. "Good team work. So, who is going back with me to stop this madness?"

I looked around at my team and sighed. I had given this a little thought and I knew I was right. But both Patty and Screamer were not going to like it.

"I think you and Ben and I should go back," I said to Laverne. It felt weird giving Lady Luck instructions, but she had asked after all.

One of her dark eyebrows actually went up at that suggestion, telling me it wasn't what she expected.

Both Screamer and Patty started to object and I held up my hand and they stopped.

"We need to keep Sherri here in case the machines come back. Screamer, you and Patty need to be here to help her through that. In the time we're gone, the slots might come back more than once."

Sherri didn't like the sound of that, but she nodded.

I turned to my boss. "Stan, you need to be here to jump to stop anyone else from getting sent back if the machines do come back again."

Stan nodded.

"That's critical," Laverne said, "because we don't have time to figure all this again."

Screamer nodded and so did Sherri.

I looked at Ben and he smiled.

"Ben knows exactly what each person looks like," I said, "so we're not trusting my memory completely. And he knows which casino they came from in this time, and when, so they can be transported to that same spot close to the time they left. That way they will never be reported missing."

Lady Luck smiled, but Patty didn't look happy.

"I'll work with my friend Johnny in the past," I said. "He was the local cop friend that helped us. He can help me pull out the right ones and keep them from going outside to the police. We'll jump them out from back in the shadows of the warehouse."

And then I looked at Lady Luck. "And you get to do all the transporting through time to where Ben says they need to go."

"A sound plan," Laverne said. "We need to get going, we're cutting this a little close."

I turned to Patty and kissed her.

She kissed me back, then said, "Make this work."

"I'll do my best," I said, smiling at her. Then as I pulled away I said, "Just have the raspberry soap ready to go."

"Oh, damn you two," Screamer said.

Sherri blushed and Patty blushed and Ben just shook his head.

It made me smile.

A moment later, Lady Luck transported me and Ben and herself ten years into the past and into the middle of a dark warehouse full of old and creepy slot machines stacked in rows that seemed to go on forever.

All of them dead, looking very much like tombstones in a graveyard in the dim light.

To one side of the warehouse was a very dangerous set of slots pulsing, sending off a light that made the big warehouse seem even more daunting and huge.

And then with a bright flash, the warehouse went completely dark.

"They jumped," I said.

"And as soon as they come back," Ben said in the dark, "we'll know if we are in the right time window."

"I hope so," Lady Luck said, her voice beside me in the dark. "We have very little margin of error."

CHAPTER EIGHTEEN
Finding Hank

WHILE THE MACHINES were gone I teleported to the front of the warehouse where I remembered a light switch being, and flipped it on.

Overhead lights clicked on, showing the gigantic size of this slot graveyard. It had to be at least two football fields long and another one wide, and the slots were stacked on shelves a good twenty feet over my head in long rows from front to back.

Laverne and Ben joined me and we went over to one side at the head of the aisle where the slots were. I pointed to a tarp that still seemed to be covering something, only if you looked hard, there was nothing there. The tarp just seemed to be floating in space. Some part of the machine never left the warehouse when it jumped.

"My gut sense is that riding on the outside of this thing isn't going to be a pleasant experience," I said. "Hank will appear under that tarp, more than likely knocked out cold."

Both Laverne and Ben nodded.

"I'm going to check the other doors to make sure none of them are unlocked or broken open from the inside," I said.

"I know he didn't go out the front door because it had a padlock on it when we arrived the first time."

"Good thinking," Ben said.

I teleported to the back of the warehouse and checked the door on the right. Secure. I jumped to the garage door and it was also secure.

Suddenly I heard Laverne in my head, *They are returning.*

I jumped back to where they were just as the machine appeared under the tarp.

There was no one in the chair under the tarp.

Damn.

The machines sat there, covered, their glow taunting me, pulling me to go sit down at them.

"Wow, that's some pull," Ben said.

"They are very powerful," Laverne said.

"I'm going to check the other door," I said.

I jumped and the instant I saw the door, I knew we were in trouble. It had been broken out from the inside.

Hank had already gotten out into the world.

I jumped back to Laverne and Ben. "He's been here," I said.

"Damn," Lady Luck said. "When was the previous jump that we know about?"

"Six hours ago," Ben said.

Laverne nodded and looked up. "Kronos, help?"

Suddenly we were back in a dark warehouse, and again through the darkness, the machine was pulsing, getting ready to jump.

"Check the door," Laverne said a moment before I vanished to do just that.

It was locked and hadn't been broken out.

"Thank the heavens," I said.

I flipped on the lights from near the back door and was about to jump back to Laverne and Ben when suddenly Hank appeared out of nowhere and hit me on the side of the head.

I had a fraction of an instant of warning from one of my superpower senses, but they were tuned to slower warnings like what I needed at a poker table.

Not someone about to hit me.

But still I managed to move just enough to cause Hank's intended blow

Some Classic Dean Wesley Smith Stories
Available at your favorite booksellers.

with an old slot handle to just graze my head.

I went down hard, but somehow stayed alert enough to say, "Hank's here!"

And then I took myself out of time, freezing Hank as he was about to smash open the back door of the warehouse.

Ben and Laverne appeared above me in the time bubble.

Ben reached down and helped me to my feet.

"You all right?" Laverne asked, frowning and looking at the side of my head like a worried mom.

I could feel I was bleeding slightly from a gash on the side of my head, and I knew for a fact I was going to have a nasty headache, but I wasn't about to tell Lady Luck herself that I wasn't all right.

"I'll be fine," I said. "My Spidey sense warned me just in time."

Ben laughed.

Laverne just looked puzzled.

"I'm going to take him back," Laverne said, nodding at Hank.

She waved a hand at him and he went to the ground like a sack of very rotten Idaho potatoes.

"Wow, nifty power," I said. "Can I learn that one?"

She laughed. "Hang around for a few more centuries and I might teach it to you. I'll tell everyone at the office we got Hank and then be back."

Then she and Hank were gone.

Ben handed me a wad of Kleenex from his pocket for the bleeding and I nodded thanks. I pressed it against the side of my head as we started walking silently up the aisle between shelves and shelves of old slot machines, a reminder of many people's dead dreams.

CHAPTER NINETEEN
Johnny Does a Double Take

LAVERNE APPEARED AS we neared the front.

"They stopped another attack," she said. "And they were happy we got Hank."

I nodded. Damn I missed Patty, even being away from her for this long seemed wrong these days. We were a team. I was stronger and smarter and much calmer with her around.

"I'm going to jump us to about a half hour before you guys start bringing people out," Laverne said.

"Too close," I said. "It took us a while to figure it out. Make it forty-five minutes."

She nodded and the next thing I knew we were standing off on the other side of the warehouse, away from the Slots of Saturn.

Something really bothered me and I looked around. Then as I heard the doorknob rattle, I knew the problem.

"Lights."

I teleported to right in front of the front door, clicked off the lights, and jumped back to a spot beside Laverne.

A moment later I heard my own voice and the lights came back on.

"Quick thinking," Ben whispered.

We stood there for the next half hour, listening to the echoes of our talk, letting me relive once again one of the most horrid times of my life. But now from what seemed like the grandstands.

If I didn't already have a headache from the hit across the head, this time-travel stuff would give me one.

Then, finally, my younger self and Patty and Screamer started rescuing people from the machine.

"Here we go," I whispered. "Ben, you watch and when you see the first one, you tell Laverne."

He nodded.

"Do you need to be touching the person to jump them back to our time?"

"No," Lady Luck said. "Ben just tell me when and where as exact as you can."

"I will," he said.

We stood in the shadows, watching as Johnny and Geneva helped the rescues from the Slots of Saturn out into the hot air and the waiting arms of ambulances and police.

"The first one," Ben said, nodding as Johnny brought her around the corner from the machines and started toward the front door, helping her along as he went.

He then told Lady Luck exactly when, right to the minute, and which casino the woman had come from and what area.

Laverne nodded. "Be right back."

The woman disappeared right out of Johnny's arms.

I stepped forward and motioned for Johnny to come into the shadows with me.

"Poker Boy?" he asked, looking very puzzled and looking back over his shoulder at the same time.

"It's me," I said.

"Geneva says you are still back there getting another person out."

"I am," I said. "That me, from this time. I'm from ten years in the future."

He started to open his mouth and I waved my hand. "We have some people the machine took from my time ten years in the future. We will just be taking those people out of your hands and getting them back to where they belong. But

you and Geneva keep this to yourselves. Don't ever tell the other me, or anyone for that matter. Okay?"

He nodded, still looking puzzled and hesitant.

"Go back to work," I said. "It is critical you and the team over there get the people out of that machine."

He nodded and turned away.

I teleported back into the shadows in another aisle so when he looked back, I would have vanished.

Laverne appeared and nodded she had been successful. But she was looking a little tired.

And that bothered me a lot.

I glanced at Ben and he was looking at her as well, looking worried.

Lady Luck should never look tired.

Ever.

CHAPTER TWENTY
A Change of Plans

AFTER THE NEXT two jumps for Laverne back to the present, she looked horrible.

When she came back after the second one, she actually staggered some.

I looked at Ben and he looked very concerned.

I needed to do something and do it fast.

"Change of plans," I said as we waited for the next one from the future. "We have eight more and we're going to hold them all here and all of us jump as a group back to my office. Can you do that?" I asked Laverne. "Just one more jump?"

"I think so," she said, her voice weak. "Kronos warned me this might not be possible. Time jumping takes a massive amount of energy. More than I had imagined, actually. More than I have ever spent in thousands and thousands of years."

That was not something I wanted to hear.

"Just sit there against those slots in the shadows and rest," I said. "Ben and I will get the other eight people rounded up."

She nodded and slid down to the ground. "Thanks."

I looked at Ben and he nodded and we went back to watching the people being rescued from the machine. In all my years, I would never have imagined giving Lady Luck orders, let alone seeing one of the most powerful gods in all the universe exhausted.

Now I just hoped she had enough energy to get us all back at once to my office. From there, Stan could take care of getting the survivors to the right places and times. Otherwise, all of us were going to be stuck in a very ugly time loop that ended with Patty and me ten years apart.

I didn't even want to think about that.

"Next one," Ben said.

The woman was being escorted by Johnny.

I stepped out into the light and walked up to Johnny, who again looked surprised to see me.

"That's one of them," I said. "We need her to wait in here with us."

Johnny nodded and I led the way into a side aisle. I quickly pulled a few tarps off of slots and put them on the concrete. "Just sit there and rest," I said to the woman. "We'll have you home shortly."

"Another one," Ben said as Geneva escorted another man from our time toward the front door.

I moved out as Johnny headed back toward the machines and motioned for Geneva to bring the man over and I had him sit on the tarp as well.

"What's going on?" he demanded.

"We're trying to get you home," I said.

He started to stand and I froze him, pulling myself and Ben out of time.

"We need help," I whispered to Ben.

He nodded. "Who can we trust?"

I knew at once who to call.

"Stan," I said, "A little help?"

Ben shook his head. "Stan can't jump through time."

"I can't what?" Stan asked, then looked at me and Ben.

"Oh," Ben said.

I had called the Stan of this time, not the future Stan.

"That you, Ben?" Stan asked, smiling. "What are you doing here? It's been a long time."

"Working on Poker Boy's team from ten years in the future," Ben said.

Stan started to open his mouth and I stopped him. "We can't tell you anything and you can't say a word that you saw us here."

"What's happening?"

"We're trying to rescue people the machine took from ten years in the future," I said.

His face went white as he instantly understood some of the problem.

"We need help with holding these people in place until the last ones get out of the machine and we can jump them all back to the future."

He nodded.

"Can you help us and never say a word, not even to Laverne."

"Does she know you are here?" he asked.

"I do," Laverne said, staggering around the corner and again sitting down, her back against a slot machine. "But I'm blocking my past self or any other gods from seeing any of this."

Stan nodded. "Not a word. What can I do?"

"Hold these people while Poker Boy and Ben round up the rest," Laverne said. "Then give me an energy boost when I try to jump us all back to our time."

"I can do that," he said, nodding.

I dropped the time bubble and Ben turned back to the steady stream of people again starting from the machines toward the front door.

Behind me the two people from the future were sitting on the floor, frozen, not moving.

Another power I really needed to learn at some point.

CHAPTER TWENTY-ONE
Too Close—Far, Far Too Close

AFTER WE HAD the seventh person sitting frozen on the tarp, I looked at Ben. "How much time do we have?"

"Thirty-seven minutes," he said. "The last one from the future should be out in fifteen minutes."

"Well," I said, "that's going to be a long fifteen minutes."

He only nodded.

"And this is cutting it far, far too close."

Again he nodded.

"Too close?" Stan asked.

"You'll know in ten years. If this works."

I looked at Lady Luck. She was still sitting on the floor with her eyes closed. But at least now she had some color in her cheeks again, as much as I could see color in the gray shadows of the thousands of dead slot machines towering around us.

Stan just kept staring at me, shaking his head.

"Sorry, can't tell you anything," I said, smiling at him. "You know that."

He laughed. "Hell, this is going to be a tough enough secret to hold for ten years."

"Well, keep it," I said, "and we'll all owe you big time."

"That we will," Lady Luck said, without opening her eyes.

After that, we stood there, watching each and every person rescued from the Slots of Saturn be helped to the front door of the warehouse and out into the heat of the day.

I forced myself to relax as much as possible. I had a hunch that Ben and I both were going to have to help Laverne make this jump to the future. I wasn't sure how, but I bet it would include feeding her energy. Last thing we would need would be to get stuck five years from now.

Finally, after what seemed like an eternity as time had slowed down and slowed down, Ben said, "That's him."

I also recognized the guy being escorted by Johnny.

I moved out into the light and took the dazed man's arm, then looked at Johnny. "This is the last one. Remember, not a word."

"You got it."

"Thanks," I said.

"I expect when the timelines catch up, you find me with a full explanation."

"I promise," I said.

I took the man over into the shadows where Laverne was now standing.

"Gather everyone together tightly," she said.

Her voice still didn't sound strong, but it sounded better than it had a little bit ago.

Stan and I and Ben did what she asked, with the eight people from the slot all in some sort of trance. I have no idea how Stan did that, but I sure wanted to know.

I'd ask him if this worked and we got back.

"Push them tight together," Laverne said. "The three of us need to be holding hands around them.

Stan helped us arrange that until I was pushed in tight against a middle-aged woman wearing far too much perfume. I just hoped I didn't sneeze in the middle of all this.

I had a hold of Laverne's hand on one side and Ben's on the other.

"Stan, stay about five feet away," Laverne said, "but focus as much energy at me as you can right now."

I could feel the energy pouring from Stan into Laverne as Stan stepped back and leaned forward and focused at Laverne.

Then, after a few moments of soaking in energy from Stan, Laverne said, "Ben, Poker Boy, on the count of three, focus every bit of energy you both have through your hands to me."

"Understood," I said, taking a deep breath.

"Understood," Ben said.

"Kronos," Lady Luck said into the air. "A little help would be appreciated right about now."

Then with Stan still focusing energy at her, Lady Luck said, "One. Two. Three. Go!"

Every ounce of energy I had I imagined it pouring through my fingers and into Lady Luck. I knew how to do that since Patty and I did that all the time with each other, but not at this level.

I felt like I was turning myself inside out. This was life or death.

There was no point in holding back any ounce of energy if I ever wanted to see Patty again.

And that thought made me pour out even more energy to Lady Luck.

Around us the warehouse vanished.

And then nothing for the longest time, or what seemed to be the longest time.

I just kept pushing energy at Laverne with all my focus.

Suddenly, we were in my office floating over the city of Las Vegas, in front of the big booth.

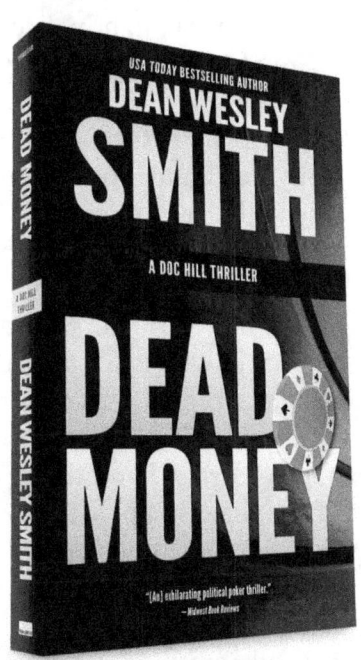

Now Available
**from all your favorite booksellers
in trade paper and electronic editions.**

The eight survivors and Laverne and Ben and I all tumbled to the ground in a bad imitation of a mass Twister Game gone horribly wrong.

The woman with too much perfume smashed me into the floor.

The only thing I remember seeing was Patty's wonderful face, panicked as she jumped out of the booth to come and help.

Then the room went black as I think I passed out.

CHAPTER TWENTY-TWO
The Magic Touch

I WASN'T SURE how long it was, but the next thing I remember was Patty stroking my forehead lightly. I could feel a little energy from her touch reviving me a little.

Every bone in my body ached.

And my head hurt from where Hank had hit me with that slot machine handle.

And I wanted to sneeze something awful.

I opened my eyes and smiled at the love of my life, who was smiling at me with those huge brown eyes of hers.

"You all right?"

"No idea," I said, honestly.

She helped me sit up.

I was still on the floor in front of the booth and Madge was hurrying in with three glasses of water.

Sherri and Screamer were sitting next to Laverne on the floor and Stan was helping Ben to sit up.

"What happened to all the people?" I managed to ask with a hoarse throat.

Patty handed me a glass of water that tasted wonderful and gave me even more energy.

"Kronos brought Burt and some of the other gods and got them all back to their right places and times," Stan said.

Laverne nodded. Then she looked at Stan with a look that I hoped someday to have her look at me with. "Thank you."

"Yes, thank you," I said, smiling at my boss.

He smiled. "It was worse in the last five hours knowing what I knew from that side, but not knowing how we got there, or if it would even work. Kronos says it did. We're back in the main time-line. Everything is reset."

Patty hugged me, smiling, and I could feel even more energy pouring through me.

"Mom," Sherri said, "Let me get you home and into bed."

Lady Luck nodded, but didn't move. "Stan, want to jump us both there and come back. Not sure if I dare risk it yet."

Stan nodded and the three of them vanished.

Patty was working to get me to my feet and into the booth and Screamer was helping Ben up from the floor when Stan appeared.

"Stan, same kind of help if you don't mind?" Ben asked.

Stan nodded and smiled. He looked at me. "We have some talking to do."

"Tomorrow," I said.

He laughed. "Tomorrow. Great work, once again."

He vanished with Ben.

"You two going to be all right?" Screamer asked.

I nodded. "After some rest."

"Great work," he said, "as always."

"You too," I said. "Tell Madge we're done for the night."

He nodded and turned and went through the door into Madge's Diner.

Outside the windows of my office, I could see the hint of sunrise starting to color the eastern hills. Below, the lights of Vegas looked wonderful.

It felt great to be home.

I couldn't remember being so tired.

And so satisfied at the same time. Especially sitting there in the booth of my office, holding Patty.

Finally, she pushed away from me and waved her hand. "You need a shower, big boy."

"Sweat?" I asked, smiling at her.

"Perfume," she said.

I stood and she held me as we headed for the door to her apartment below.

"You might need to soap me up some," I said, smiling at her. "I'm pretty tired."

"Raspberry soap?" she asked, smiling back and hugging me.

"Of course," I said. "Just like the first time ten years ago."

"I don't think either one of us has the energy to do what we did that first time ten years ago," she said, kissing me as we went through the door and into her wonderful apartment.

And, of course, she was right.

But the next night we certainly tried to repeat what we had done ten years before in that wonderful shower with that wonderful-smelling soap.

And we honestly came pretty darned close.

And in sex and raspberry soap showers, pretty darned close is pretty darned nice.

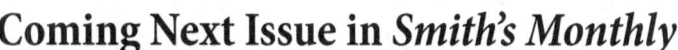

Coming Next Issue in *Smith's Monthly*

THE TAFT RANCH

A Thunder Mountain Novel

#1...October 2013

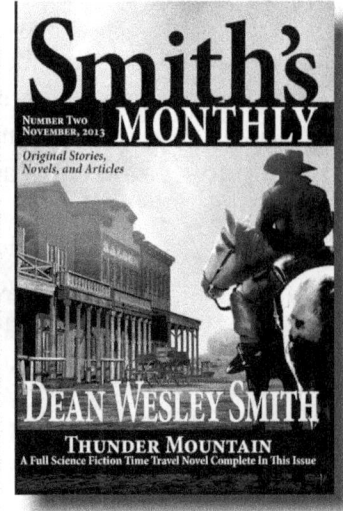

#2...November 2013

#3...December 2013

#4...January 2014

#5...February 2014

#6...March 2014

#7...April 2014

#8...May 2014

#9...June 2014

#10...July 2014

#11...August 2014

#12...September 2014

#13...October 2014

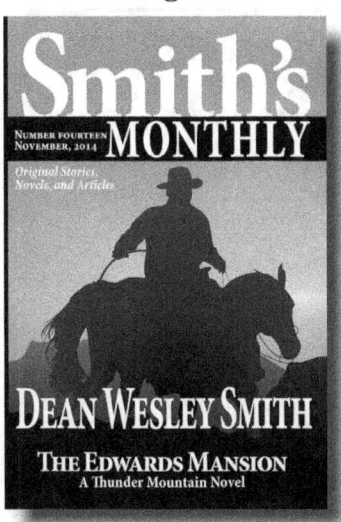

#14...November 2014

#15...December 2014

#16...January 2015

#17...February 2015

#18...March 2015

#19...April 2015

#20...May 2015

#21...June 2015

#22...July 2015

#23...August 2015

#24...September 2015

#25...October 2015

#26...November 2015

#27...December 2015

Thank You!!

I would like to thank the following wonderful people who support my blog and my work through Patreon. Your support is very important to me. Thanks!

Betsy Wilcox	Erick Lindman
Irette Y. Patterson	Christopher Ridge
Kathryn Rooney	Terry Mixon
Wendy Lee Maddox	James Husun
Jamie Curierre	Sherman Cox
Chris Cousino	Chong Go
Jane Lawson	Maria Grace
Shantnu Tiwari	Grondpom
Miguel Angel Alonso Pulido	Fen
Nancy Hendrickson	Robin Brande
Ryan M. Williams	J.R. Murdock
Jacob Proffitt	Kathleen McClure
Marian Goldeen	Gunnar Gunderson
Gary Speer	F.I. Goldhaber
Megan Bryce	Mary Jo Rabe
Michelle Tatam	John Kilgallon
Ann Tucker	Dave Hendrickson
Kari Wolfe	Jabberwocky
Albert Lemke	Eric Goebelbecker
Stacey Larson	Marsha Kessler
Diane Darcy	Scott Gordon
Krystle Jones	Martyn Folkes
Kari Gallagher	John
T. Thorn Coyle	Cj Lehi
Tasha Turner Lennhoff	Brenda Smith

www.ingramcontent.com/pod-product-compliance
Lightning Source LLC
Chambersburg PA
CBHW081154170626
46813CB00009B/3192